DATE DUE

THE GHOST,
THE WHITE HOUSE,
AND ME

THE
GHOST,
THE
WHITE
HOUSE,
AND ME

Judith St. George

HOLIDAY HOUSE / NEW YORK

WITH LOVE TO TWO SISTERS,
EMILY AND HANNAH

Library of Congress Cataloging-in-Publication Data

St. George, Judith
The Ghost, the White House, and Me / by Judith St. George.
p. cm.
Summary: When eleven-year-old KayKay Granger learns that the White House is haunted
and uses that knowledge to play a prank on her family, she lands in big trouble with her
mother, the United States President.
ISBN-13: 978-0-8234-2045-2
[1. Children of presidents—Fiction.   2. Family life—Washington (D.C.)—Fiction.
3. White House (Washington, D.C.)—Fiction.   4. Ghosts—Fiction.   5. Washington
(D.C.)—Fiction.]   I. Title.
PZ7.S142Whi 2007
[Fic]—dc22
2006046705

CONTENTS

CHAPTER ONE

IN WHICH VISITORS ARRIVE

The White House! Me, KayKay Granger, the daughter of the president, living in the White House! Inauguration Day was only two weeks ago, so it's still hard to believe. But when I look around my bedroom at the wall-to-wall carpeting, walk-in closets, floor-to-ceiling windows, and outside at the acres of trees and fountains—right in the middle of Washington—it begins to sink in.

To tell the truth, I feel like I've moved into a museum that I'll never call home. I miss our old house with its creaky floors and whistling radiators, the big old kitchen where I tried out recipes from *Cookbook for Kids,* and the library window seat where I could close the draperies around me and no one would know where I was or what I was doing.

What I was doing was writing. I'm a secret writer. I graduated from diaries in third grade to plays, and from plays to mysteries. Now that I'm in sixth grade, I'm starting a mystery set in the Rocky Mountains. I haven't worked out the whole plot yet, but I've got some ideas in the back of my head. It helps to keep what I'm doing a secret so I don't feel any pressure to hurry up and finish the way I do with homework.

It's hard to keep anything a secret around here. Everyone, especially my Secret Service agent, Tom, knows where I am from morning till night. And today my sister, Annie, and I are having a perfectly good Saturday ruined. I was going to work on my mystery, and Annie wanted to go ice-skating with a friend. But President Donald Williamson—I mean, ex-President Williamson— and Mrs. Williamson are coming to the White House for lunch with Mom and Dad, *and* they're bringing Borden, their know-it-all grandson. Mom told Annie and me that we have to entertain Borden. Ugh.

Borden Williamson, who goes to Ward-Driscoll School like Annie and me, is the smartest kid in my class, maybe in the whole school. But he's a big talker and doesn't let anyone forget it. Actually, I can't think of anything that Borden Williamson could say or do that I'd care about.

I groan. "Some morning this is going to be, and not just morning. Borden S. Williamson's hanging around for lunch, too."

Annie is polishing off a cranberry muffin left over from breakfast. "The S. probably stands for Stuffy."

Annie's two years younger than me, but I have to admit she's smarter. And always ready with a comeback. I'm usually the wordsmith, but I can't think of anything insulting starting with *s* except *stupid* or *silly* or *spacey* and Borden isn't any of those.

"I could have been ice-skating right now." Annie twirls, spins, and dips as if that's the way she skates, which it isn't. "I don't see why I have to do this anyway. Borden's your friend, not mine."

I snort. "My friend? Oh yeah, I forgot. Borden and I are best friends."

Annie finishes her muffin and wipes her mouth with the back of her hand. "You said it, not me."

It's time to head out. Before Mom went down to the State Floor to pick up the Williamsons, she told Annie and me to be waiting by the elevator in exactly fifteen minutes . . . or else. Annie and I never argue with Mom's ". . . or else." But I hate to turn off my computer. I click to SLEEP. There, at least my mystery can doze until I get back.

The elevator's a good hike down the Family Floor hall from our bedroom. The hall doesn't have a single chair or sofa to curl up in. It's like a museum, loaded with antiques, paintings, knick-knacks, chandeliers, and flowers. The Family Floor is usually crowded with Secret Service, maids, flower arrangers, repairmen, and I-don't-know-who-else running around. But for some reason everything's quiet today, even our footsteps on the new-smelling carpet.

Annie and I are almost at the elevator when Dad comes hurrying after us. "I'm coming! I'm coming!"

That's Dad, always late.

Dad runs his hand over his head to pat down what hair he has left. "I was supposed to be down-stairs to welcome the Williamsons. Don't either of you tell your mother I was watching golf and for-got the time."

"How much?" Annie's big on picking up stray change.

"Oh, so now you're into blackmail?" Dad puts on a mock horrified expression. "That depends on how much you'll give me for not spilling the beans about you two spying on our dinner party last night."

I'm sure to be the villain if Mom finds out Annie and I were sneaking around. "Why don't you two call it even?"

"Fine with me." Dad straightens his tie and smiles. "I hear the Williamsons' grandson is com-ing. Is that Borden of the boring Bordens?"

Annie and I laugh. Dad is short and pudgy with a great smile. He can always get Annie and me to laugh—even if we're not in a laughing mood, like now. When I was three, he was such a perfect Santa Claus, I got confused that maybe he was the real Santa Claus. Dad looks on the upside of everything, which makes him a soft touch for almost anything Annie and I want to do. He's like our own personal Santa Claus.

But Dad turns thoughtful. "Something interesting happened last night, girls. I woke up with a start and couldn't get back to sleep. I don't know what startled me, but as I lay in bed, I sensed an undercurrent of energy that runs just under the surface here in the White House."

Dad's thinking can go off in crazy directions. An undercurrent of energy woke him up? That's pretty heavy, even for Dad. Maybe life in the White House has freaked him out the way it has me.

Annie's forehead wrinkles with that worried look she gets. "What do you mean?"

Dad shrugs. "I can describe it as a feeling I have that the White House is haunted."

"Haunted? By ghosts?" Annie's question is a squeal. Annie was, is, and probably always will be, scared of her own shadow.

I'm into mysteries, for sure, and I like Edgar Allan Poe stories, but I'm a practical person and have much too much common sense to believe in ghosts. Besides, how could the White House be haunted with Secret Service agents coming and going all the time? "No way, Dad."

Dad shakes his head. "Not that kind of haunted. I mean the White House is haunted by history. Consider the incredible amount of history embedded in the very bones of this place. Talking about history, KayKay, I just finished a book I think you'd like, biographies of all the presidents. I'll lend it to you. Maybe it'll give you an idea of what I'm talking about."

That sounds like a book I'll probably never read. "Thanks, Dad."

Annie isn't about to give up on the ghosts. "The man I saw on the day we moved in might have been a ghost. I was watching out the window at the movers bringing our stuff in, and one mover acted really weird. He was bald, super tall, and thin with a strange sort of beard and no mustache. He came in the south entrance not carrying anything, and I waited and waited but I never saw him come out. And he didn't get off the elevator on our floor with furniture, either. Doesn't that sound funny, Dad? The White House is more than two hundred years old. Why wouldn't ghosts hang out here?"

The question is for Dad, but I answer. "Because there's no such thing as ghosts, that's why. Your ghost could have been the guy in charge who just told everyone else what to do and didn't have to do any work himself."

Dad gives Annie a quick hug. "KayKay's probably right, Annie. I promise you don't have to worry about ghosts in the White House."

Annie isn't convinced. "I don't know how you can promise that. When KayKay and I took that tour of the White House like you asked us to, the man said there's always been a tradition of ghosts in the White House."

By now Dad is probably sorry he ever mentioned the White House being haunted. "Tradition in that sense means legends, Annie, just stories, you know, like myths, not facts."

I sigh. Now Annie will be on a ghost kick.

Even at nine years old, Annie's a hold-on-just-a-minute worrier. In our last house Annie was afraid to go upstairs alone after dark, so I had to go with her. It's not that I'm crazy about the dark myself, but I had to show Mom and Dad that I was braver than Annie. And more dependable.

Before Annie can start in again, we're interrupted by the sound of the elevator humming up to the Family Floor. The door slides open and Mom steps out, followed by the Williamsons, Borden, and Caitlin, one of Mom's Secret Service agents.

Mom frowns at Dad, but he pretends not to notice as he shakes hands all around. "President Williamson . . . Mrs. Williamson . . . so good to see you . . . and Borden. Welcome."

Mom takes over. "President Williamson, I think you know our daughters, Katherine and Ann. Girls, President and Mrs. Williamson, and I'm sure you know Borden from school."

I've met President Williamson before, and I certainly know Borden. As I shake hands with the Williamsons, Borden pulls out a handkerchief, not even a Kleenex, and cleans his glasses. I know it's to save the two of us the ordeal of having to shake hands, though no handshake suits me fine.

Mrs. Williamson gives Annie and me a sugary

smile. "If I didn't know better, I'd think you two Granger girls were twins." She seems pleased with herself, as if she weren't the hundredth person to tell us that.

Annie and I both have brown eyes, blondish brownish straight hair, and ears that stick out a little too much. We're almost the same height except that Annie is taller, which makes me crazy. I'm short and skinny for eleven, while Annie is really tall for nine. Mom calls her "sturdy," a word that makes Annie crazy, but then Mom has always told it like it is.

And we're different in just about every other way, too. Annie avoids trying anything new. Not me. I'm an organizer and more gung-ho-charge-ahead. That's why I like working out a mystery plot step-by-step and clue-by-clue, while Annie would never read anything that might be scary, like a mystery. Sometimes Annie and I go at it, but mostly we get along, and I love her as my baby sister.

Knowing how we hate to be taken for twins, Dad comes to our rescue. "KayKay's named Katherine for my mother, who's petite. Annie's named Ann for Margaret's mother and has the same Brooks family height. As a baby, Annie called Katherine KayKay, and she's been KayKay ever since."

I'm KayKay to just about everyone but Mom and my teachers. Mom called me KayKay until I was about six, then she started calling me Katherine. When I turn thirteen, I plan to drop the KayKay forever, though I'm not sure what I like better. Someone told me that years ago, a president's son was known as JohnJohn, and I don't want to suffer the same little kid double-name fate for life.

Mom cuts off the family-history talk. "We'll be in the East Sitting Hall, girls. The Ping-Pong table is set up for you in the third-floor Solarium. Harris will bring you soft drinks. Just tell him what you want."

"Madam President." Suzanne, Mom's personal secretary, appears from out of nowhere with her red notebook like she's been doing ever since she started working for Mom three years ago. "Could you please sign these letters, ma'am?"

I can see Mom is annoyed though she tries to

hide it. She signs the letters, and Suzanne disappears as silently as she appeared. "I apologize for the interruption, Donald. That should have been taken care of earlier."

"No apologies necessary. Don't forget, Madam President, we may come from different political parties, but I know all too well that home and office are one and the same." President Williamson emphasizes the Madam President. Madam President! The title surprises me every time I hear it.

Of course, Borden has to step in with his opinion. "Having your own movie theater, tennis court, and two swimming pools isn't anything to sneeze at. And you can thank Grandie for having the indoor pool built. But what I liked best is ordering any food you want, like Chef Toni's devil's food cake."

I'm tempted to point out that by the looks of him, Borden must have eaten his way through his grandfather's entire four-year term, but I know Mom would kill me. Besides, Dad and Annie are both big into eating and think it's a first-class perk, too.

There are probably other perks, but I'd rather be back in our old house and old neighborhood, where Annie and I could come and go. Dad says our family is about to have the all-time adventure of our lives. Mom says that adventures are all well and good, but Annie's and my top priority is school.

No one likes the thought of adventure more than me. But Dad's haunted-by-history White House doesn't make it. As for Annie imagining she saw a ghost, that doesn't make it, either. All in all, I can't believe any kind of adventure is waiting for me in this huge, white, open-to-the-public museum.

CHAPTER TWO

IN WHICH A TRAGIC TALE IS TOLD

As soon as Mom and Dad head down the hall with the Williamsons, I organize the Ping-Pong game. I'm a good organizer. Annie should appreciate the fact that I get things done and stop calling me bossy. At least I don't start every day with a list of Things to Accomplish, the way Mom does.

"Okay, let's get going with the Ping-Pong. Borden and I will play first, then Annie can play the winner." Annie's better at Ping-Pong than I am, just like she is at almost every sport.

Borden shakes his head. "I don't play Ping-Pong. It's a dumb game. We'll bowl."

Annie and I give each other a look. I've never bowled, not even once. Neither has Annie. But Mom made it clear we're to be polite to Borden, so that's that.

"We can take the elevator down to the basement." Borden has definitely taken over.

"The basement? We have to go to the basement?" Annie never went in the basement of our old house unless I was with her, and truthfully, it *was* dark and spooky.

Borden looks at Annie as if she's crazy. "Yes, the basement. Do you think we're going to bowl in the Oval Office?"

I shrug my shoulders to let Annie know she doesn't have a choice.

Borden leads the way, with me keeping up and Annie tagging behind. But Mom's secretary, Suzanne, is waiting by the elevator. How did she get past us without our seeing or hearing her? She doesn't bother with any hi's or hello's. "Chef Toni plans to serve a one o'clock lunch to your parents and the Williamsons. She wants you three to eat at noon sharp."

Suzanne's showing up at the elevator is *so*

Suzanne. Annie calls her the Pale Phantom, and it's a perfect name. She's like a phantom, popping up in unexpected places without warning. And she's pale, with pale skin, pale blue eyes, and pale blonde hair. Her clothes are pale, too, like the pale yellow pants suit she has on today. Though she's stick-thin with a little wispy voice, she has great long feet that don't match the rest of her.

Mom says Suzanne is super efficient and she counts on her. But when Mom isn't around, she treats Annie and me as if we're Public Enemy Number One and Two. She makes it clear that she thinks we're both hopelessly spoiled.

"Okay," I tell her. "We'll be there."

Suzanne nods and leaves. No hello's and no good-bye's, that's Suzanne.

We step into the elevator and head down. Having to use an elevator to get from one floor to another is a pain, though it's a cool elevator. The bottom half is wood paneling, with wallpaper on the top half and a chandelier in the ceiling. I'm always on the lookout for book ideas and this elevator would make a great setting. *The elevator door silently glides open to reveal the body of a beautiful woman.* Mmm, I don't think I'll have a murder in the story I'm writing now, but maybe sometime I'll write a murder mystery and use that as my opening sentence.

Three flights down and we're in the basement. Annie must be relieved. It's the neatest basement I've ever seen, and all lit up. The bowling lane looks professional, with shiny waxed wood, ten pins, and a mechanical picker-upper. Chairs and a scorepad are already in place. It creeps me out that unseen, unknown somebodies seem to know what we Grangers are going to do before we do it.

Like me, Borden's no good at sports, so I'm surprised that he's an expert bowler. He probably spent hours practicing. I'm not sure I'd come down here alone like that. Dad said another White House legend is that a secret tunnel runs from Pennsylvania Avenue into the White House basement. If Annie ever heard about a secret tunnel, she'd never step foot in this basement, all lit up or not.

Annie catches on to bowling faster than I do. I'm hopeless, especially when know-it-all Borden keeps giving me advice.

Borden: "Take four steps before you let go of the ball."

Me: "One, two, three, four." Down the gutter.

Borden: "No, no, release the ball, don't throw it."

Me: "One, two, three, four, release." One pin falls.

Borden: "You're not aiming. Aim between the first and third pin."

Me: "One, two, three, four, aim and release." Another gutter ball.

I give up.

"You can keep score, KayKay. Not that math has ever been your specialty." Borden's just full of charm.

I half watch Borden and Annie bowl but don't keep score. If Borden doesn't like my math, then he can keep score himself. As for Annie, I can't help being annoyed that she's enjoying herself.

As I sit there watching, I mull over what I should have said to Borden: "I may not be much in math, but I'm a hundred percent better writer than you are," would do it. Last year in fifth grade I wrote a play for my friends and me to put on that was titled *Who Stole the $300?* It was about the twenty-fifth reunion of our class. The heroine solves the mystery as to who stole three hundred dollars cash from our teacher's desk twenty-five years ago, money that the class was going to use for a trip to the planetarium. The culprit? The school principal. Everyone loved it, even the principal.

The mystery I'm working on now takes place in a Colorado lodge where our family was supposed to have gone skiing last Christmas. It never happened. After the election Mom was too busy to go, appointing her Cabinet, working on her Inaugural Address, and a million other things.

That's the story of all our trips. Mom never takes time off so we end up not going anywhere. In my mystery, I plan to describe the most elegant ski lodge I can dream up. First, though, I have to figure out the plot so that all the clues mesh together at the end.

"Katherine."

I'm so into thinking about my story, I jump at the sound of my name.

It's Suzanne standing in the doorway. She

glares at me, her hands on her skinny hips. "Where have you been? Chef Toni asked me to find you and I've been searching high and low. You were due upstairs for lunch at noon. Harris finally remembered that Borden likes to bowl. You're supposed to be playing Ping-Pong in the Solarium."

Suzanne snaps at me as if it's my fault. I'm already half-annoyed. Now I'm totally annoyed and not about to apologize. "Borden wouldn't play Ping-Pong. It was either bowl or nothing."

Suzanne doesn't give an inch either. "Chef Toni is keeping your lunch warm." She stalks off, probably to tell Mom that I whisked Borden away without telling anyone.

We take the elevator back upstairs. Our Family Floor has a little alcove off the kitchen where Annie and I eat when Mom and Dad have guests. Instead of the formal Family Floor dining room, it's a regular kind of breakfast nook, which makes it my favorite place to eat. The three of us pick up our lunches from Chef Toni and sit down.

We had part-time help in our old house, but here at the White House we have full-time help with a capital F. Annie and I don't ever have to set the table or do the dishes. Actually, I like to hang around kitchens trying out easy recipes, but this kitchen is so small, there isn't room for more than one person or maybe two at the most. Still it's got everything: a professional range and stove, and granite counters, with French copper pots and pans hanging from hooks.

Though Chef Toni is a tiny redhead with freckles who doesn't look all that strong, she swings a mean cleaver and carts around filled-to-the-brim pots. She's such a good cook, she must be French. Toni's probably a nickname for Antoinette.

Lunch picks up my mood. Annie and I earlier put in an order for grilled hot dogs, fried onion rings, cole slaw, double-fudge brownies à la mode, and a mixture of iced tea and lemonade called an Arnold Palmer. Like Dad, we both love onions, and it didn't take long for us to find out we can have onions any way we want—fried, boiled, creamed, soaked in dressing, on top of, in, and under everything. I don't give the White House a lot of top grades, but like Borden said, it's A+ in the food department.

Borden eats three hot dogs, passes on the onion rings, asks Chef Toni for potato chips, and then polishes off two brownies. He takes a long slurp from his Arnold Palmer and then looks at his empty plate. "I really miss this food. I miss the White House stories, too, the good and bad presidents who hung out here and the way the White House is always in the middle of the action."

Good night, Borden sounds like Dad. What gives that they're both caught up in this place as if it had a life of its own?

Borden tries to change his expression to modest, which isn't easy. "Though I plan to be a doctor someday, there's always the chance I might end up here. John Adams and John Quincy Adams and the Bushes—George H. W. and George W.—were father-son presidents. The only grandfather-grandson presidents were William Henry Harrison and his grandson Benjamin. If I'm ever president, Grandie and I would be the second grandfather-grandson ever."

I almost choke on my brownie. "You as president? You've got to be kidding."

Annie laughs. "Be sure to wait until I'm old enough to vote . . . for somebody else."

Borden's ego seems indestructible. "Neither of you know anything. I bet you can't even name all the presidents."

Borden acts so superior, like he knows more about the White House than anyone else. Dad's an American history professor and Mom's been in politics forever, so they know more about the presidents than Borden ever dreamed of knowing. But he's right. I couldn't possibly name all the presidents and don't want to.

Annie's on the same wavelength. "The only president I care about is Mom. President Margaret Brooks Granger is the best."

Annie's right. Mom is good. She's a good speaker, good at meeting people and remembering their names, good at running meetings, good at making political appointments, good at raising money, good on TV. As senator, she got a major privacy bill passed. Her nickname was Ms. Privacy, and with that, she was on her way to being president.

Don't get me wrong. I'm proud of Mom. But

sometimes she isn't such a great mom. She was old—forty-one—when I was born and almost forty-four with Annie. Even though she was Massachusetts attorney general, she found time to feed the ducks with Annie and me in the summer and take us sledding in the winter. Then Mom ran for the U.S. Senate and won. All of a sudden, she got too busy to spend time with us, and then running for president sent her right out of our orbit. When she did make an effort to come to an after-school game or a music program, it was as if she did it just to cross off one more chore on her list of Things to Accomplish.

Dad's different. Dad taught at Harvard until he resigned to support Mom's campaign for president. He was home between classes a lot more than Mom, so he showed up at school programs whenever he could. Dad doesn't act superintellectual the way most people think professors act. He puns, tells jokes, and teases Annie and me.

I can't imagine Borden cracking a pun or even telling a joke. Now he wipes mustard off his chin, though the glob of mustard on his glasses doesn't seem to bother him. "Since you're living in the

White House, you'd better get with it. You've heard of Abraham Lincoln, I hope."

Annie fakes a puzzled look. "Abraham Lincoln? Mmm, wasn't he in that movie about aliens?"

Borden doesn't even smile. "Aren't you the funny one."

I can tell that Borden's going to plow ahead whether we want to hear what he has to say or not. "Okay, so what about Abraham Lincoln?"

Borden drains his drink. "Abraham Lincoln haunts the White House. And he's always polite. He knocks before entering a room."

Annie looks stunned. "That's what Dad said! He said the White House is haunted. I think it's haunted, too."

I laugh. "C'mon, Annie, that's not what Dad said. He said the White House is haunted by *history*."

Borden ignores both of us. He lowers his voice. "President Theodore Roosevelt said that Lincoln's spirit haunts the White House, and he was right. When Franklin Roosevelt was president, a secretary saw Lincoln putting on his boots. President

Ronald Reagan's daughter spotted him standing by a window. Even Chef Toni says she thought she saw him once."

Borden glances behind him as if to make certain nothing—or no one—is there. I can't help looking around, too, for what I don't know, certainly not ghosts. Ghosts are for people who believe everything they see on TV.

Poor Annie sits frozen in her chair. "You know that moving man I told you about, KayKay? He had a beard like Abraham Lincoln and he was really tall and thin and—"

Borden interrupts, dropping his voice even lower. "Last year Grandie let me spend a night in the Lincoln Bedroom." As Borden leans in closer I bend in closer, too, in spite of myself. He pauses. "There's no television or radio in the bedroom and I didn't have anything to read, so I went to bed and just lay there. I finally fell asleep, but something woke me up. It was a knock on the door. I heard the clock strike two, followed by another knock on the door. I turned on the light. That's when I saw it . . . Lincoln's reflection in the mirror."

I shake my head in disbelief. "Abraham Lincoln's reflection?"

Borden looks at me as if I'm a moron. "Of course Abraham Lincoln's reflection. I just kept staring at the face until it faded away. Now if that isn't a ghost, what is?"

"Abraham Lincoln's ghost, that's what it was. See, KayKay, that moving man I saw could have been Abraham Lincoln's ghost." Annie's voice is a whisper.

This is a stupid conversation. "Take it easy, Annie, you said yourself the moving man was bald, and Abraham Lincoln wasn't ever bald. Besides, there's no such thing as ghosts."

Borden's eyes narrow behind his glasses. "Oh yeah? Lincoln himself believed in ghosts. In April 1865 Lincoln said he'd had a dream where he heard 'pitiful sobbing.' In his dream he followed the crying to the State Floor, where he saw a coffin surrounded by soldiers and weeping mourners."

I don't like the sound of this. "A coffin? Here in the White House?"

Borden nods. "Right in the middle of the East

Room. Lincoln asked who was dead in the White House. 'The president'—a soldier told him—'. . . killed by an assassin.' Lincoln said he didn't sleep for the rest of that night. Within two weeks Abraham Lincoln was dead—assassinated. His coffin lay on a platform in the East Room just like in his dream. For three days thousands of people lined up to view his body."

I glance at Annie. She's glued to her chair and still looking stricken.

It must be catching. All of a sudden, I realize how quiet the Family Floor is. Usually there are voices, a door closing, a phone ringing. Now there's only silence, even from the kitchen. And the dark winter day has grown even darker. Looking out the window, I see the White House flag flapping in a freezing rain.

All the mysteries I've read, plus the one I'm writing now, must be getting to me. And it's weird to be only down the hall from the Lincoln Bedroom. It's even weirder to be sitting just above where Lincoln's body lay.

Why did Borden tell us all this, anyway? He was probably just trying to show us how brave he is and scare us at the same time. I'm not like Annie, but would I ever have the guts to sleep in the Lincoln bedroom? I'd have to think that over.

It didn't take much thought, after all. *I'm* in the White House now, not Borden, and if he can have a real adventure, so can I. When have I personally ever had an adventure? Never. If I spend a night in the Lincoln Bedroom, I could dream up my own Abraham Lincoln ghost appearance to tell Borden that would make his Lincoln's face-in-the-mirror seem pathetic. A real adventure may be waiting for me here in the White House after all.

CHAPTER THREE

IN WHICH A DOOR
IS OPENED

Annie and I are supposed to deliver Borden to his grandparents at three o'clock in the Diplomatic Reception Room. That's the family and guest entrance on the Ground Floor. It's an oval-shaped room, like the Blue Room above it on the State Floor and the Yellow Oval Room above that on our Family Floor.

These three oval rooms are like those fake Easter eggs that have little windows to peek in and see tiny scenes. But with the oval rooms, it's possible to get inside the scenes instead of just looking in.

Mom, Dad, and the Williamsons are already waiting when Annie, Borden, and I show up. Two West Wing office staffers are out in the hall, and I can see by Mom's forced smile that she's itching to get back to work even though it's Saturday. Yesterday I heard her talking on the phone about some problem in Chile, and maybe that's why she's so antsy. I know how she feels. I can't wait for the Williamsons to leave so I can check out the Lincoln Bedroom.

No one hangs around. Mom gives her presidential half wave, half salute, and the three Williamsons are through the door, down the stairs, and into their limousine. That does it. Borden is over and done with.

Mom hurries off, all business, while Dad sits down to wait for a professor friend of his from Harvard, who's due any minute.

I'm off and running. "I'm going to take a look at the Lincoln Bedroom. Are you coming, Annie?"

Dad looks up. "Now you're talking, KayKay. If Borden Williamson is responsible for your sudden interest in history, I'll have to take back my boring Borden remark and thank him."

Should I tell Dad that White House history is the furthest thing from my mind? I guess not. Instead, I give him a big smile. "Right, Dad. Well, are you coming, Annie?"

Annie shakes her head. "Not now. I'm going to wait here with Dad."

She doesn't fool me for a minute. Borden and his Lincoln ghost have freaked her out.

I hurry along the hall where portraits of ex-First Ladies line the walls: Pat Nixon, Betty Ford, Rosalynn Carter, Jackie Kennedy. Wouldn't you know that the women's portraits are down here on the Ground Floor instead of upstairs on the State Floor with the men? I like to kid Dad that his portrait will hang here someday with the other First Ladies, and he always retorts that he's counting on me to pick out his gown for the sitting.

What people should call Dad has been sticky. First Gentleman? First Spouse? First Husband? In our old house we had a toilet that never worked right. Dad suggested his title should be First-Person-to-Call-When-the-Toilet-Overflows. He got a unanimous no vote on that one.

I take the Ground Floor marble stairs two at a time up to the State Floor. From there, I head for the Grand Staircase off the Entrance Hall. It's the staircase that Mom, Dad, and their official guests use to make their entrance as the Marine Band plays "Hail to the Chief." I'm still trying to get used to Mom being the chief chief.

Portraits of our latest presidents look down from the Grand Staircase wall—Ronald Reagan, George H. W. Bush, Bill Clinton, George W. Bush, Donald Williamson. It's as if they posted themselves as watchdogs and don't like me running up THEIR Grand Staircase.

Voters who didn't want a woman president probably won't want Mom's portrait on the State Floor wall, either. Still, if they try to stick her portrait downstairs with the First Ladies and not up here with the presidents, I'll have a hissy fit they'll never forget. I may complain about Mom and living in the White House, but I'll stand up for her, anytime, anywhere.

As I run up the stairs I begin to have doubts about going into the Lincoln Bedroom by myself. Annie would have been no help, but at least she would have been another live body. I just wish I didn't know that Lincoln's coffin had lain in the East Room for three days.

Once I get to the Family Floor, I head toward the big fan-shaped window at the east end of the hall that's near the Lincoln Bedroom. When I reach the door, I hesitate and then push it open.

I see right away why stories about Abraham Lincoln's ghost are big around here. The rest of the White House is lit up like a Christmas tree, but only one old-fashioned desk lamp is turned on here. It hardly sheds any light and long shadows stretch across the room.

I take a step in and then stop, my hand on the doorknob.

Above the slap-slap of icy rain on the windows, I hear a scratching noise that sounds like giant fingernails running down a blackboard. Or something clawing at the windows to get in. Heavy draperies block most of the two windows, and my eyes aren't used to the faint light. I stand frozen, debating whether to go in or run. Then as I adjust to the light I see that a couple of tree branches are scraping against the windowpane. Letting out a breath of relief, I make my way over to the bureau and turn on a lamp by the bed. But it doesn't give any more light than the desk lamp.

No wonder Borden made a big deal about sleeping here. I slowly look around, wondering why anyone would want to fill a room with such awful furniture. Carved birds, flowers, and bunches of grapes decorate the headboard of the bed that towers over everything like some huge beast guarding the room. Me sleep in that bed? I'm small and the bed is enormous. Even Annie and I together wouldn't take up much space.

Scattered around the room are old-fashioned chairs and a sofa that all look stiff and prickly. In the middle of the room, there's a marble-topped table with horrible legs of carved, ugly, long-beaked storks with a bird's nest filled with eggs connecting the four legs at the bottom.

And then I see it. On the far side of the room over by the windows is a wardrobe with a mirror on each of its two doors. That has to be where Borden said he saw Lincoln's face. I see myself reflected, but I see another face, too. Lincoln's face! I squint. No, it's not Lincoln. It's a woman's face.

I take a terrified step back and wait for the face to fade away like it did with Borden. But it doesn't fade. Wait a minute, the face is framed. I spin around. The mirror is reflecting a portrait of a woman that hangs on the wall behind me. Mrs. Lincoln? I have no idea. Breathless, I sink into the nearest chair.

The chair tilts backward, startling me. It's a rocking chair. As I try to regain my balance my hand brushes against a small statue on a table. A tiny, somber, lifelike Abraham Lincoln is seated in an armchair.

The little statue does it. But as I get up to leave, three papers under glass catch my eye. Good night, it's the Gettysburg Address, hand-written and signed *Abraham Lincoln, November 19, 1863*, on the last page. Even I've heard of the Gettysburg Address.

I hear a cough behind me. What am I doing here, trespassing in Abraham Lincoln's room? I turn around, not letting myself think who, or what, I might see.

It's Annie. She's standing in the open door-way, panting as if she'd been running. "Dad and his friend dropped me off on their way to Dad's study."

Annie's breathlessness gives me a shot of courage, and all of a sudden, I decide to spend a night here. I'm a mystery writer, aren't I? This room is what mysteries are all about: dark, gloomy, mystical, otherworldly. Sleeping here would give me perfect firsthand research into the inner heart of a mystery.

"Annie, come in. I've got a great idea. You and I can sleep overnight here, like Borden did. If Borden can do it, so can we."

Annie doesn't budge. "I wouldn't sleep here for a hundred dollars. Besides, I keep thinking about that moving man with the beard. What if it was Abraham Lincoln?"

Give me a break. I can usually get Annie to change her mind, but this is going to take more convincing than usual. "Come on, Annie, you saw him at a distance, didn't you? I mean, men with beards and no mustache are everywhere." I tried to think of someone with a beard and no mustache. The only one I could come up with is Mr. Weeks, our school custodian. "Look at

Mr. Weeks, Annie. He's got a beard and no mustache."

"Yeah, but Mr. Weeks is short and fat, and has tattoos."

I sigh. Annie is so literal. "I don't mean Mr. Weeks looks like Abraham Lincoln. I'm just saying lots of men have beards and no mustache. Hey, Borden got me sort of steamed up, too, with all that knock-on-the-door and face-in-the-mirror stuff, but he'll make up anything to get attention. C'mon, Annie, spend the night here with me. I'll watch out for you the way I used to when I took you upstairs in the dark."

"Forget it. This room is totally creepy."

Annie has a point, but since I have to talk her into this, I'm certainly not going to tell her that the room gets to me, too, especially that tiny Abraham Lincoln statue. The only reason I want Annie to sleep here is because I think we'd have a fun adventure together. Wanting her with me doesn't have anything to do with me being afraid to sleep here alone. No, absolutely, positively, definitely not . . . at least that's what I tell myself.

CHAPTER FOUR

IN WHICH A REQUEST IS DENIED

I'll ask Dad first if Annie and I can sleep in the Lincoln Bedroom. I wait until his friend leaves before I check in with him. He usually goes along with almost anything Annie and I want to do.

"It would be so great, Dad, if Annie and I could sleep in the Lincoln Bedroom for a night."

This time Dad doesn't go along. "I can't give you the okay on that, KayKay. You'll have to ask your mother. But I'm really pleased, though not surprised, that you're getting a sense of history living here in the White House. By the way, I left that presidents book I told you about on your bedside table."

It's too bad Dad doesn't feel he can give permission. Mom is big into rules and regulations and not as free with her yeses as Dad is, which means I'll have to find just the right moment to spring the question on her. Maybe tonight.

I lay in wait, knowing she has to come into her bedroom to change her clothes before her dinner guests arrive. Mom's bedroom door opens with a bang, and she hurries in. That's not a good sign. I give her a big smile anyway. "Hi, Mom."

She rushes past me to her closet. "Oh, hello there, Katherine. What is it, dear? I'm running late and have to change. Is Janelle around? Could you find her, please?"

Janelle is Mom's hairstylist, and it isn't going to help my case that I saw Janelle waiting impatiently by the elevator about ten minutes ago. Mom is already out of her dress and putting on another when I give her the bad news. "I think Janelle's gone home. She left a little while ago."

Mom's head pops out through the neck of her dress. "Oh no, Suzanne must have forgotten to tell her to stay on tonight. Well, I've been in charge of my own hair before, I guess I can cope tonight. Did you want something, Katherine? I'm rather pressed."

This is no time to ask a favor. The trouble is, as far as I can see, there never is a good time. Mom can't help being busy, busy, busy, and I understand that. But she's never busy with just Annie and me. Maybe when she gets used to being president, she won't be so rushed all the time. "I didn't want anything. I just wanted to say hi. I've hardly seen you for three days."

Mom reaches over and pats my cheek. "I know, dear, and I'm sorry. But we can look forward to Sunday night. Uncle Matt and Aunt Lisa are coming for dinner, and we'll be just family. Then we can talk all we want."

Mom pulls a shoe box out of her closet and changes shoes. There isn't much point in me hanging around. At least Sunday night sounds promising. Mom is crazy about Uncle Matt and she'll be in a good mood. Their father died when Mom was thirteen and Uncle Matt was seven, and Mom used to take her baby brother to school and watch out for him until she went off to college.

Now Uncle Matt is a doctor, a medical researcher who has discovered cures for diseases I never heard of. He and Aunt Lisa don't have any kids—so as far as Uncle Matt is concerned, Annie and I might as well be his.

Borden, who's always talking about being a doctor, would probably like to meet Uncle Matt. But Uncle Matt has a great sense of humor and I wouldn't stick him with Borden. Uncle Matt is always good for games and jokes, though some of the ones he pulls on Annie and me aren't all that funny.

Uncle Matt's worst trick was when he found an old baby picture of Annie and me under a Christmas tree wearing Santa Claus hats and nothing else. He had it blown up like a poster and hung it in his living room last year at a family Christmas party, where it got lots of laughs from everyone but Annie and me.

Still, I love Uncle Matt. I'm even going to put him in my mystery—with his name changed, of course. He'll swoop down a mountain in a helicopter to save my heroine. Though I haven't figured out yet why my heroine needs saving, it will make a dramatic ending.

So far my mystery is still a secret. Annie would just give me a hard time, Dad would nag me to let him read it before it's even finished, and Mom, well, Mom would probably put it on her pile of Things to Accomplish and never get around to it.

On Sunday night dinner is served exactly at seven in the small President's Dining Room on the Family Floor where presidents' families eat. We never eat in the big dining room on the State Floor called the Family Dining Room that's used only for White House dinners. Did someone reverse those names, or what?

Chef Toni has cooked Mom's favorite dinner: mushroom soup, veal rib roast, rosemary potatoes, and glazed carrots. And Chef Toni remembers to give Dad, Annie, and me our own iced bowls of green onions with her special dressing. I figure the veal roast combined with seeing Uncle Matt will mellow Mom into a yes for the Lincoln Bedroom.

But of course Uncle Matt has to have his fun

with Annie and me first. "So, are you two little princesses spending your days learning all the royal requirements like curtseying and receiving the attention of handsome young princes?"

Annie laughs. "Sure, Uncle Matt, I've had ten proposals so far."

I chime in. "Yeah, but any prince who wants to marry us has to slay a dragon first."

Aunt Lisa puts her hand on Uncle Matt's arm. "You shouldn't tease the girls, Matthew. It's such an unattractive trait." She smiles at Mom. "I'm sure it's just because he's glad to see Katherine and Ann."

Mom tries to smile, but it's pretty weak. Mom liked Uncle Matt's first wife, Tracey, but after their divorce he married Aunt Lisa, never a Mom favorite. "Matt's been a tease ever since I can remember, Lisa. I always found it one of his charms."

Uncle Matt laughs. "That-a-way, Sis. Or I guess I should call you Madam President."

Mom shakes her head. "Not with family, Matt. After all, I can remember changing your diapers."

Aunt Lisa probably doesn't like that. She's all

proper behavior and saying-just-the-right-thing. Like Mom, I can't understand why funny, nice Uncle Matt married her.

Uncle Matt doesn't seem to mind the diaper comment. "Okay, how about telling us about school, then? Are you two president's daughters the high muckety-mucks of Ward-Driscoll these days?"

I can answer that. "Tom, my Secret Service agent, and Gloria, Annie's Secret Service agent, go to school with us every day. It's like having another backpack to lug around. At least nobody pays any attention to them. Borden Williamson had a Secret Service agent when his grandfather was president, but Borden never let up on how important he was, which got to be a big bore."

Uncle Matt looks puzzled. "I'm confused. These agents are so small, you keep them in your backpack?"

Annie takes over. "See, they drink something before school that makes them small like Alice in *Alice in Wonderland* so they fit in our backpacks. Then after school they drink something else that makes them regular size again."

Everyone laughs, even Aunt Lisa, and we all get down to the business of eating.

There's so much talk during dinner, I wait until Harris from the Steward staff serves our salads and there's a quiet moment. "Mom, I have an idea. We study the Civil War this year, and Annie and I are here in the same White House where Abraham Lincoln lived, so how about the two of us spending a night in the Lincoln Bedroom, and if we write a report about it, I'm sure we'd get extra credit, and besides, it would give Annie and me a sense of history, and that's what Dad is always nagging us to get."

Whew, one breath got me through the whole thing.

Before Mom can answer, Uncle Matt turns to Dad. "Hey, it sounds to me as if KayKay might follow you into a history career, Professor John. To tell the truth, I'm still hoping that she'll follow in *my* footsteps."

To kid Dad, Uncle Matt calls him Professor John. Dad no longer has classes, but he still lectures at colleges around the country. Dad kids Uncle Matt back by calling him Doc Matt.

Though Dad doesn't plead my case, he tries to score a few points for me, and I know he's talking more to Mom than to Uncle Matt. "KayKay certainly doesn't have to follow in my footsteps, Doc Matt, but I'd be thrilled if she and Annie took advantage of living here to dig into the history of the White House, and that includes the Lincoln Bedroom." He turns to me. "You found that book I left for you, didn't you, KayKay?"

It's sitting on my bedside table, unopened. "Yes, thanks, Dad."

Though writing, and not history or medicine, is in my future plans, I'm encouraged. But then I notice Mom's famous frown and I see my chances fade. I'm right. "I'm sorry, Katherine, but my answer is no. And dear, please sit up straight."

I give it another try. "Borden Williamson's grandfather let him sleep there, and Borden didn't even live in the White House, like we do. He just visited a lot."

Mom doesn't waver. "What Borden Williamson did doesn't concern me, Katherine."

I keep going just in case Mom decides to change her mind. "But just think of the extra credit, Mom. And maybe I'll write an article for the school paper."

Now Mom is getting annoyed. "There will be no sleepover for either you or Ann in the Lincoln Bedroom. Period."

Annie is usually too busy eating to talk much, but this time she sticks her foot in her mouth instead of food. "I wouldn't sleep in that bedroom anyway. Who wants to mess around with a ghost?"

I kick Annie under the table. She's supposed to be the smart one, so how come at just the wrong moment she comes out with something so dumb?

Even worse, Uncle Matt picks right up on it. "Ghost? You mean Abraham Lincoln's ghost?"

I put on my most sincere look. "That's just Borden Williamson showing off, Uncle Matt. He says a knock on the door in the middle of the night woke him up and he saw . . . I mean, he *thought* he saw Lincoln's face in the wardrobe mirror."

My sincere look doesn't do it. Uncle Matt slaps the table. "Now that's the kind of history I go for. How about letting me stay there for a night, Margaret? All I've ever seen are second-rate ghosts that no one's ever heard of, never a famous one. Abraham Lincoln would be a top-of-the-line sighting."

Mom laughs. Uncle Matt can always get Mom to laugh, but I can see by the way she tilts her head that she's about to turn Uncle Matt down. Before she can, Aunt Lisa turns to Uncle Matt. "You're putting your sister on the spot, Matthew. I'm sure it's not up to her anyway."

That's all Mom needs to give Uncle Matt the go-ahead. Aunt Lisa hasn't learned yet that no one ever tells Mom what she can, or cannot, do.

I'm right again.

As Harris clears off our salad plates Mom puts her hand over Uncle Matt's. "Next Saturday night is quiet around here, Matt. I'll arrange with Suzanne for you to spend the night. But don't count on any extraterrestrial visitations."

Uncle Matt jumps up from his chair and gives Mom a hug. "Margaret, being president has done you good. And next Saturday is perfect. Lisa and I leave the following Monday for Europe to tour medical facilities." He turns to Dad. "Hey, Professor John, is this big sister of mine special or what?"

Though Dad nods, he isn't smiling. "I don't always agree with every decision, but she's special, all right."

I know Dad is with me, for what little good that does. Mom's like two people, president and mom, and right now she's in her president role. I can't believe she turned me down flat and then let Uncle Matt sleep in the Lincoln Bedroom. What's going on? She thinks more of her brother than of me, her own daughter? It isn't fair. Tears start into my eyes, but I refuse to let them fall.

Harris brings in the chocolate rum cake dessert, which Mom ordered because she knows how much Uncle Matt likes it. As everyone digs in, I get to thinking. Suzanne may think Annie and I are spoiled, but Uncle Matt is the one who's spoiled. I'm serious about sleeping in the Lincoln Bedroom. I need the experience so I can step into the world of the unknown, while Uncle Matt just thinks it would be a fun thing to do. Besides, I'm the daughter of the president, not just the brother, and I should be allowed to spend the night there, too.

Dad wants me to get into the White House

mode, while Mom won't even let me give it a try. Okay, if that's the way it's going to be, I'll just have to dream up some way to scare Uncle Matt the night he's in the Lincoln Bedroom, something so terrifying, he'll be sorry he ever asked.

CHAPTER FIVE

IN WHICH A PLOT
IS HATCHED

After Sunday night dinner Mom, Dad, Uncle Matt, and Aunt Lisa watch a new movie in the East Wing projection room. I'm still cross at Uncle Matt for asking, and being allowed, to sleep in the Lincoln Bedroom. Now the four of them are watching a movie while Annie and I are stuck doing homework.

I always do my homework in our eating alcove. I like the cooking smells and the clatter of Chef Toni bustling around with her pots and pans. As I lay out my books and papers cinnamony smells come out of the kitchen and I feel better. I stick my head around the corner.

Chef Toni looks up and grins. She knows what I'm about to ask. "My blue ribbon, best-of-the-show apple-cinnamon breakfast rolls."

"Mmm, smells good. And dinner was great."

"Thanks, KayKay."

Usually I bring my mystery notes along so that I can jot down any ideas that might come to me. Not tonight. My thoughts are on what Annie and I can do to terrorize Uncle Matt. With my mind drifting, my homework takes forever, but I finally finish . . . all but the math. At least I've made up my mind that scaring Uncle Matt with Lincoln's ghost is our obvious goal. But I haven't a clue as to how we can do it.

I open my math book. We're into beginning algebra this year, and it's my sworn enemy. As I glare at my math hoping it will reveal its secrets to me, Harris walks by on his way to the President's Dining Room with a tray of tomorrow morning's silver and china.

Mom, who is always at me to stand up straight, uses Harris as an example, and Harris does stand as straight as an arrow. Trust Dad to know that Harris has worked in the White House for thirty years and has a daughter at Yale and a son in medical school.

I give a wave. "Hi, Harris, how are you at math?"

He stops. "Really good . . . as long as I have a calculator."

"Me too."

Harris puts down his tray, leans over, and looks at my book. "That's not for me. If you need help, you should ask your friend Borden Williamson. Borden knows more about math than anyone. And he knows more about the White House, too. That boy's a superbrain."

Borden . . . Borden . . . Borden. I never paid any attention to Borden before, now all of a sudden, he's in my face. I'd better set Harris straight. "Well, actually, he's not my friend or anything that I'd ask him for help."

It's not that I'm jealous of Borden being so smart, or want to be an expert on the White House like he is, but he doesn't live here, I do. And my take on living in the White House isn't like Borden's anyway. With having to be polite to everyone who shows up, look halfway decent all the time, and have no privacy, I feel hemmed in.

Harris picks up his tray and leaves. I struggle awhile with the math and then give up and put all my effort into coming up with a plan to scare Uncle Matt. My language arts teacher says I'm a creative thinker, and I am, so why am I having so much trouble?

When I told Annie that it was payback time for Uncle Matt, she came up with an idea right away. "You could phone Uncle Matt after he's asleep, disguise your voice, and pretend you're Abraham Lincoln."

Me sound like Abraham Lincoln? I don't think so. Still, I don't want to discourage Annie if she's willing to join the program.

As it turns out, my ideas aren't any better than Annie's. I first thought of hiding in the Lincoln Sitting Room next door to the Lincoln Bedroom, and making ghostly noises in the middle of the night. But I don't know what ghostly noises are or how to make them. Then I thought of using Morse code, which I know because Uncle Matt taught it to me last year. I could knock a message on the bedroom door in Morse code. But why would Abraham Lincoln signal in Morse code?

Besides, Uncle Matt would guess right away it was me.

Mmm, Morse code. My mind goes to my own mystery. Maybe I'll have two villains and they'll communicate through the ski lodge wall by Morse code. I quickly write the idea down on the edge of my math paper. Changing the direction of my brain must have charged my batteries. When I tackle my math again, I finish it.

The next day, Monday, is like any other Monday. School!

Tom and Gloria, our Secret Service agents, drive Annie and me to the Ward-Driscoll School and stay with us all day. My Secret Service code name is Sparky, for Sparkplug. Annie is Mrs. Goodspeed. I don't know why, maybe because she's a fast runner. Or maybe someone named Mrs. Goodspeed is a serious worrier like Annie. I've asked Tom how the Secret Service picks names for people, but he said he didn't know.

Because Borden was guarded when his grandfather was president, the Ward-Driscoll kids are used to seeing agents around. Though Borden thought it was great having his own agent, I can't get used to having Tom tag along with me all day.

I glance over at Borden in math class and look, really look at him for the first time. He's bent over working on a problem. His glasses have slipped down his nose, so that even from four desks away, I can see how smudged they are. His usual button-down Brooks Brothers shirt has worked itself halfway out of his pants, with the cowlick in his hair standing on end. He probably starts out the day all together, but by nine o'clock he's falling apart.

The whole class gets stuck on one algebra problem, which makes me feel better because I don't get it, either. But Borden does. When his hand shoots up, Mrs. Davies asks him to show the class how it's done on the blackboard. Borden explains it better than Mrs. Davies did in the first place. Harris is right. Borden is a super brain.

Harris also said Borden knows more about the White House than anyone. And he does. Maybe Borden could help Annie and me out. The way he loves to show off and be the big expert on the White House, he'd be sure to come up with an idea to fool Uncle Matt. And it would probably make him feel important. I'll talk it over with Annie.

On our drive home from school, Annie and I huddle together in the backseat. I put my finger to my lips to indicate we have to whisper. "Okay, Annie, we have four days left until Saturday, and we don't have one good idea about scaring Uncle Matt. We'll have to resort to desperate measures."

"Like what?"

"Like asking Borden Williamson for help."

Annie's yelp says it all. I try to reassure her. "Borden can be a geek, all right, but he's a smart geek. Besides, we can't think of anything ourselves, can we?"

Annie has to agree.

For once, on Tuesday I can hardly wait to get to school. I track Borden down in the lunchroom, which isn't hard, since he always sits alone at the same table. I know he loves Chef Toni's food, but now he's stuck with school food. I almost feel sorry for him as he looks at his tray of creamed chipped beef on toast, grayish steamed broccoli, limp lettuce with yellow dressing, and a packaged cookie, and then over at my half an avocado stuffed with shrimp salad, cinnamon rolls from yesterday's breakfast, an onion-and-cucumber salad, and peach cobbler.

Borden's glasses are practically steaming with envy as I go into my prepared speech. "Borden, I've got a problem maybe you can help me with."

He snickers. "You have more than one problem. I bet you got all ten algebra problems wrong today."

Actually, I got three right, but I'm not about to tell Borden I had seven wrong. Instead, I hand him my cinnamon rolls. "Here, I'm not very hungry. You can have these."

Borden is delighted. "Hey, great!"

Good, now Borden's in a positive mood for the rest of my speech. "My uncle Matt is going to sleep in the Lincoln Bedroom Saturday night, and Annie and I want to scare him with Lincoln's ghost. But we don't know what to do or how to do it. We figured since you know so much about the White House, you'd probably come up with some good ideas."

With luck Borden will knock off talking about math and move on.

Borden doesn't even mention math. Instead,

he acts interested. "Is your Uncle Matt the famous Dr. Matthew Brooks?"

"Yeah, I guess he's famous."

Borden smiles, and I notice what straight white teeth he has. "He's famous all right. I read an article by him in a medical journal. I'd really like to meet him." Hint, hint.

I hedge. "Maybe. So, what do you think? Do you have any ideas?"

Borden finishes both cinnamon rolls before he says anything. "Nothing comes to me right now, but I'll think about it. Saturday? That's not much time."

He's telling me?

Borden gives a chuckle. "One bit of advice is don't run around the White House after midnight. President Ford took his dog out late one night, but when he wanted to get back in, the elevator was turned off. He went up the stairs, but the Family Floor doors were all locked. He had to pound on the walls to get the Secret Service to let him in."

I'm amazed. This is boring Borden? The story isn't half-bad. I don't know anything about President Ford, but if he told that story on himself, he must have had a sense of humor.

If I felt sorry for Borden with his awful lunch, I feel really sorry for him in language arts. Everyone has to read their book reports out loud to the class. That's one class where Borden never volunteers. And when it's his turn to read, he stumbles through a mishmash of incomplete sentences and mispronunciations. All of a sudden, it occurs to me that maybe Borden is dyslexic. Like the kids who need special help, he's never around during study period. Maybe he's getting special help with reading.

When I finish my turn, Mr. Lang comments, "Good work, Katherine." It's like Borden's and my math and language arts roles are reversed.

If Borden wants, I could give him help. But he isn't in school the next day. Maybe he doesn't want to face the kids in our language arts class. With time running out, I can't wait another day. I phone him at home that night.

Borden's voice is hoarse when he answers. "Hey, thanks for calling, Kay. I have a sore throat, but I'll probably be in school tomorrow." Even hoarse he sounds so pleased that I called, I don't have the heart to tell him I only wanted to ask if he'd come up with a plan for Annie and me.

I try to sound upbeat. "Well then, I'll see you tomorrow. We can meet at lunch period in the cafeteria."

I keep my fingers crossed that he'll show up. Sure enough, the next day he's in homeroom. What a relief! I catch his eye and give him a thumbs-up. He nods, smiles, and returns the thumbs-up.

Borden's already picked up his lunch and is waiting for me by the time I get to the cafeteria. As he starts in on his insipid-looking tuna and noodle casserole I open my lunch: a ham, turkey, swiss cheese, and red onion sandwich on rye, deviled eggs on the side, ending up with spice cake. I made the Seven-Minute Seafoam icing and am proud of it, if I do say so myself. Chef Toni showed me how to beat the egg whites and brown sugar over boiling water for seven minutes, add cream of tartar and vanilla, and beat hard until it was smooth and glossy.

To encourage Borden, I pass over my piece

of cake, painful as that is. Besides, I owe him one for calling me Kay on the phone instead of KayKay.

He pushes his Jell-O aside and tackles the cake. "Say, thanks." He sounds genuinely grateful.

At last Borden gets started. "When I was home sick yesterday, I saw a TV special on Richard Nixon. When Nixon was president, he taped phone calls, meetings, and conversations, but never told anyone that he was taping." Borden pauses to finish his cake.

I force myself to nod encouragement. "Mmm, that's interesting."

"Those tapes ended Nixon's presidency. He resigned." Borden runs his finger around his plate and licks it. "That's the best icing I ever ate."

"Thanks." So far I've given Borden my cinnamon rolls and spice cake and I'm still nowhere. But I am surprised that a president resigned. I didn't know any president had ever resigned. Maybe I'll look up Nixon in my still-unopened presidents book.

Borden pushes his glasses back up his nose.

"The tapes got me to thinking. You could buy the CD of Lincoln's Gettysburg Address that they sell in the Visitor Center. Download the CD into your iPod, set its alarm clock, and then put your iPod into a dock—"

I interrupt. "Wait a minute. I don't have an iPod dock."

"You're kidding." Borden looks at me as if I'm deprived.

I *am* deprived. "No, I'm not kidding. But I think Dad has one. Wait a minute, I know he does. I remember when he got it. I'm sure he'd let me borrow it."

"Good, you'll need one. After you dock your iPod, program it to play the speech good and loud in the middle of the night, like two or three o'clock. Then hide the dock somewhere in the Lincoln Bedroom where your uncle will be sure to hear it. The wardrobe's probably the best place. Is that a plan or is that a plan?" Borden smiles a self-satisfied smile.

If I believed, like Dad, that there's some kind of undercurrent of energy flowing through the White House, I might not go along with this on the chance it could blow up in my face. But what's the problem? I'm a down-to-earth writer. I don't believe in undercurrents any more than I believe in ghosts. As far as I'm concerned, Borden has the right to be pleased with himself. His plan to scare Uncle Matt is brilliant.

CHAPTER SIX

IN WHICH PREPARATION IS ALL

As soon as Annie and I get home from school on Thursday, we head for the kitchen to hit the cookie jar. Because Mom is busy in the West Wing, and Dad left today for San Francisco on a lecture tour, we have to check in with Mrs. Bruning, better known as Mrs. B. Mrs. B. keeps an eye on Annie and me after school, and though Mom calls her a housekeeper, in reality she's a babysitter. As if I need a babysitter!

Probably Mrs. B. is in the library, my favorite room. The library's wood paneling, leather chairs, deep, red carpeting, and hundreds of books make it look like a book lover's heaven. I've already mentally filed it away as a dramatic setting for another mystery after I finish the one I'm working on. *Detective Forsyth gathered all the formally dressed houseguests into the mansion's handsome library. He seemed sure of himself, as if he already knew who the culprit was.*

Of course, I'm not exactly ready to start a second mystery, since I'm still outlining the plot of my first one. So far I have my heroine, Madison Blake, staying at the elegant ski lodge in Colorado with her best friend, Lori Anders. A crime takes place that Madison will solve—a jewel theft is what I'm thinking now.

But there's no time for writing today. Annie and I have a job to do. And it's all working out. With Dad away, we can use his new dock without having to answer a lot of questions. First, we'll pick up the Gettysburg Address CD from the Visitor Center down in the East Wing, then download the speech onto my iPod, dock the iPod, set it, and we're all prepared.

Sure enough, Mrs. B. is in the library knitting what looks like a ten-foot-long yellow scarf. Mrs. B.

is a big knitter. Maybe she wants to project a grandmotherly image. She certainly looks like a grandmother, with flyaway white hair, glasses, blue eyes, pink cheeks, and teeth that are too perfect. Because she's always so bright and chipper, she reminds me of a plump, hippety-hop sparrow.

With Mrs. B. curious about every move we make, keeping our moves secret is going to be a challenge. Luckily, Mom thinks that Mrs. B. is sharper than she actually is. As a babysitter, Mrs. B. is okay, especially since she watches *Afternoon Talks with Dr. Ken* on TV from five to six every day. If Annie or I want to do anything questionable, five to six is when we do it.

Mrs. B. keeps on knitting as she greets us with a smile. "Well, girls, isn't it wonderful to have school all over until tomorrow? When I was your age, afternoons were my favorite time."

I try to sound casual. "We love the afternoon, too, don't we, Annie? Say, Mrs. B., we'll be right back. We're going down to the Visitor Center to pick up a CD I need for school."

I make sure not to lie. When we study the Civil War later this year, I can take the CD to school.

Mrs. B. puts down her knitting. "That isn't necessary, dear. I can phone for anything you want, and they'll send it up."

Uh-oh, that's no good.

My mind races to come up with some excuse. "That's okay, Mrs. B. Afterward, Annie and I are going to—to—" I'm practically stuttering but don't come up with anything.

Quick-thinking Annie steps into the breach, though she slightly fudges the truth. "Swimming. KayKay and I are going to take a swim in the pool. I have to practice so I can pass the test for my swim badge."

Perfect, though I happen to know Annie's already earned her swim badge.

Mrs. B. picks up the phone. "Well, all right. I'll put in a call for your agents to meet you at the elevator."

Oh no, that isn't much better. But we can't object. If only it weren't such a hassle to be by ourselves.

As Annie and I stuff our swimsuits, flippers, goggles, and towels into our backpacks I congratulate her. Because Annie has been dragging her feet about this project from the start, I try to boost her up. "Wow, you really saved the day with Mrs. B., Annie."

Annie's too sharp for her own good. "You're just saying that to keep me happy. After today I'm through with this whole Lincoln Bedroom thing."

I've got my work cut out for me, but not now. "Hey, whatever you decide is okay with me."

We stick our heads in the library, wave to Mrs. B., and head for the elevator. Tom and Gloria are waiting for us.

The four of us get in the elevator, I press the GROUND FLOOR button, and the door closes. I go into my routine. "I have to pick up a CD of the Gettysburg Address for school. We can put it on Dad's credit card." Dad would never complain if he thought Annie and I were improving our minds.

Gloria laughs. "I guess school hasn't changed much since my day. Every time Lincoln's birthday rolled around, out came the Gettysburg Address."

The East Wing is mobbed. Even in freezing weather like this, tourists have lined up around the block to come in the East Gate at the Ground Floor level. They swarm all over the Ground Floor, checking out the Library and the Vermeil, China, and Map rooms. From there they tour the East, Green, Blue, Red, and State Dining rooms on the State Floor before leaving by the North Entrance.

Does anyone else in the world live in a house where more than a million strangers troop through every year? And what if all these people heard stories about Lincoln's ghost and stampeded up to the Family Floor to check out the Lincoln Bedroom?

That's dumb. I'm turning into a worrier, like Annie. The Secret Service wouldn't let anyone on our floor.

On the other hand, almost all the tourists have cameras. Above all, Annie and I don't want to be photographed. If Mom saw our picture in the newspaper or caught us on TV, she'd never give up until she found out what we were up to.

As Tom and Gloria clear a path through the Visitor Center for Annie and me there's an immediate silence.

"Those are the Granger twins," I hear a man whisper.

The woman with him shakes her head. "They're not twins. Still, seeing them together like that, you'd certainly think they are."

Annie and I are too recognizable. Someone who knows us, like a teacher or a friend of Mom's, might spot us and say something to Mom. I give Tom a push. "Tom, please get the Gettysburg Address CD. And hurry."

Annie, Gloria, and I wait in the elevator. As soon as Tom joins us, he hands me the CD, which I slip into my backpack. Lovely silence greets us as the elevator takes us down to the pool. We just suffered through the noisy, nosy public side of the White House. Now we're in the quiet, private, no-tourist side, where no one knows where we are.

The usual White House unseen army has been at work. The pool thermometer is at a just-right eighty-two degrees, and the nearby hot tub is bubbling away. If only I could get my mind off that CD.

After we swim and fool around for half an hour, I'm ready to get out, but Annie challenges me to a race. Even though I'm not a great swimmer, to keep her happy, I agree. Tom and Gloria start us off. Halfway down the pool it occurs to me that Dad might have taken his dock to San Francisco. At the thought, I swallow water, choke, and Annie wins by almost half a length.

That's dumb. Dad would use his headphones while traveling.

On our way back up to the Family Floor in the elevator, I flip my wet hair over my shoulder, making sure water sprays on Annie. Being beaten by a nine-year-old in a swimming race, or any kind of race, is unacceptable. As Annie turns around and shakes her wet hair all over me, Tom steps between us.

"You know, there used to be another indoor pool. President Franklin Roosevelt had it put in." Tom is acting as if he doesn't know that Annie and I are about to come to blows. "Roosevelt was paralyzed and couldn't walk without help, though the public never knew it. That pool was covered up, but your friend Borden's grandfather had this new pool built three years ago."

How come everyone calls Borden my friend

just because he came to the White House for one day? It's ridiculous. But I'm not going to argue. Besides, I want to know why the public couldn't figure out that the president was paralyzed. "How could a president keep it a secret that he's paralyzed?"

Tom shrugs. "Times were different then. The media respected Roosevelt's privacy, and there was no TV to record his every move. And the White House staff never let on that he always used a wheelchair."

Times must have been different, all right. The media writes, discusses, analyzes, and photographs every step we Grangers take. The media . . . the White House staff . . . what if Annie and I pull off this Abraham Lincoln ghost-scare on Uncle Matt and someone on the White House staff leaks it to the media? I can just guess what Mom's reaction to that would be.

I tell myself that anyone working in the White House, especially Secret Service agents, must take some kind of pledge not to talk about the First Family. But the possibility of a leak nags at me all the way up in the elevator.

After Tom and Gloria drop Annie and me off on the Family Floor, we report to Mrs. B. She's still knitting, and the scarf looks even longer than when we left. I check the library clock—4:43. That gives Annie and me time for more cookies before Mrs. B. checks in with her program. But as we head for the kitchen Mrs. B. calls out to ask where we're going.

Mrs. B. should be Mrs. C. for Mrs. Curious. We can't make a move without her wanting to know what we're up to. "We're just going to the kitchen," I yell back.

Chef Toni hasn't returned, and the kitchen is empty.

Annie gives me a sly, sideways look as she munches on a cookie. "I saw what you're writing on your computer. It's a mystery, isn't it? You probably think you're going to get it published."

I can hardly believe my ears. "You went into my computer? How could you? That's my private space."

Annie finishes one cookie and starts on another. "Everyone knows that nothing on a computer is ever private."

I'm furious. "That's not true, and you know it. Going into my computer is like . . . like . . . it's stealing, that's what it is. You're stealing my privacy. It's like opening my regular mail and reading it."

Annie grins. "I never read your regular mail, KayKay, because you never get any. Besides, you thought it was okay to spray me with water in the elevator. I figure I owe you one."

"You don't owe me one. You already sprayed me back."

Annie doesn't raise her voice. "You started it."

I bring out the ultimate weapon. "Yeah, and I'll end it, too. I'll tell Mom what you did, and she'll let you have it. You know what a fanatic she is about privacy."

Panicked, Annie stops chewing. "You'd never tell Mom. I know you wouldn't."

Now I have her. "Who's to stop me? And I'll wait until Mom's in a big hurry or she's distracted by something important so she'll be even more annoyed."

"That's not fair, and you know—"

"Hi there, KayKay, Annie." Chef Toni's voice from the doorway startles me.

I try to pull myself together. "Oh hi, Chef Toni."

Annie turns to go, but not before she throws out one last zinger. "I'll see you back in our room, Nancy Drew."

That *Nancy Drew* is the last straw. I have to bite my lip to keep from snapping back in front of Chef Toni. Instead, I thank her for the cookies and head out into the hall, where I try to cool off.

It's a couple of minutes past five by the time I get it together. I left the CD in my backpack, so I don't have any choice but to go in our bedroom. Annie's on her bed reading one of her animal stories.

Annie closes her book. "I'll come with you."

She wants to make up, but I ignore her. She's only acting friendly so I won't tell Mom on her. But friendly doesn't make it. Still, I'll need Annie's help putting everything together. Okay, I'll be nice for now. "Go check on Mrs. B. and make sure she's watching TV."

"Okay." Annie runs off.

While she's gone I put the CD in my computer and download the speech into my iPod.

The funny thing is that whenever Annie and I

have a fight, neither of us stays mad for long. And I know that my I'll-tell-Mom threat scared her enough so that she won't go into my computer again. I have a hunch she'll never mention my mystery again, either, for the same reason.

Annie catches up with me. "Mrs. B. is glued to *Dr. Ken.*"

For some reason, we both tiptoe into Dad's bedroom. Dad chose Mrs. Williamson's sitting room for his bedroom, but his beat-up old desk, cracked leather chair, computer, printer, fax machine, copier, papers all over, and books stacked on the floor make it look more like an office. And they don't do much for Mrs. Williamson's rose-colored carpet, pink-flowered wallpaper, and pink-and-white-striped draperies.

Dad keeps his dock by his bed. No problem. I unplug it and we take it back to our bedroom. My hands are almost trembling as I set my iPod in it and scroll down to play the Gettysburg Address. "Four score and seven years ago our fathers brought forth, upon this continent, a new nation, conceived in Liberty, and dedicated to the proposition that all men are created equal . . ." it begins, and ends: ". . . we here highly resolve that these dead shall not have died in vain—that this nation, under God, shall have a new birth of freedom—and that this government of the people, by the people, for the people, shall not perish from the earth."

Wow! That's real writing! Short as it is, only two or three minutes, it makes what I write look pathetic.

But Annie is worried. "That speech is so short, it will be over before it wakes up Uncle Matt."

I didn't think of that. "I'll turn the volume to high."

But does the voice sound like Abraham Lincoln? Though Dad once said that Lincoln had a high-pitched voice, the CD voice is deep and throaty, like an actor trying to sound like a president. At least it's a man's voice and not me faking it.

Next we set the iPod alarm for 2 AM and then turn it off. Neither of us is very mechanical and we take our time making sure we've done everything right. We'll turn the alarm back on when we hide the dock in the Lincoln Bedroom Saturday afternoon. Any earlier and someone might find it.

I can't wait to tell Borden that thanks to him, we're ready to go. But the next morning in school,

Borden hands me a paper bag in homeroom before I have a chance to tell him. He has a pleased-with-himself look on his face. "President Teddy Roosevelt had a slogan: *Preparation is all.* I've adopted that slogan myself. That's why I'm giving you these new batteries for your dock. You don't want the speech to fade out or not play at all."

It never occurred to me that the dock might need batteries, but of course the wardrobe wouldn't have an electrical outlet. With all my complaints about Borden, he's come through on every detail. Like Teddy Roosevelt, Annie and I are now totally prepared for Saturday night with a plan, materials . . . and a victim. I don't see how anything can possibly go wrong.

CHAPTER SEVEN

IN WHICH A
MUTINY ERUPTS

It's Saturday afternoon, and I'm at my computer working on my mystery. I've finally worked out the plot. A wealthy countess, dripping with jewels, has just arrived at the same exclusive ski lodge where Madison and her friend, Lori, are staying. Two days later, during a blizzard when everyone is stuck inside, the countess lets out a scream. Her jewels are missing. It's the turning point of the plot, just the way the Gettysburg Address is going to be the climax of Uncle Matt's stay in the Lincoln Bedroom.

But a problem's come up that makes it hard for

me to concentrate. One of Annie's Christmas presents was ice-skating lessons, and she's at the rink this afternoon. What if she's late and Uncle Matt arrives before she gets home? I can't risk that he might catch us setting up the dock in the wardrobe.

When I hear Mom's voice in the hall, I hurry out. She'll know when Uncle Matt is due to arrive. Mom is talking to Suzanne, who's taking notes in her red notebook. These past few days Mom has been on a different plane, and Dad says it's because she's still coping with some problem in Chile. She gives me one of her fleeting political smiles, which means she doesn't see me. I understand why she's out of focus on the home front, but it would be nice if she'd direct one of her milewide family smiles at me, her daughter. Suzanne doesn't even look up. All of a sudden, I have an idea. I'll model the snooty countess in my mystery after Suzanne. Brilliant!

"Please check to make sure that drinks will be served in the Diplomatic Reception Room at seven, with dinner at eight," Mom tells Suzanne.

Suzanne nods. "Yes, ma'am."

As I start to speak, Mom holds up her hand to stop me. "And I'd like to know what kind of table arrangements the Protocol Office is making, if you'll check on that, too, please. It's important that everything goes off without a hitch."

Suzanne nods again. "Yes, ma'am."

As soon as Suzanne leaves, Mom turns to me. "Come in, Katherine. I'm free for a few minutes. And dear, do stand up straight."

Mom says that so often, I hardly hear her.

Mom's sitting room is half-Mom and half-not-Mom. Her warm antique furniture clashes with the bright pink-and-green flowered wallpaper and striped pink-and-green draperies. Pink may have been Mrs. Williamson's color, but it's not Mom's. She said she never dressed Annie and me in pink, because it was her least favorite color. I wonder how long it will be before Mom trashes the pink.

Now that I think about it, I wouldn't mind trashing Annie's and my barf green bedroom rug, with the same deadly green in the wallpaper and draperies. When we moved here, I counted on having a room to myself, but Annie didn't want to be alone and begged me to share a bedroom like we always have. I haven't told her yet, but I'm going to ask for my own bedroom decorated in my favorite color, aqua, at the same time I drop the KayKay nickname.

Mom stretches out on her chaise lounge and kicks off her shoes. "Let me catch my breath. I just had tea with local day care directors, followed by punch with National Merit Scholarship winners. I'm about to float away."

When isn't Mom at some meeting or another? I sit down on the end of the chaise. "Mom, what time is Uncle Matt coming tonight?"

Mom puts her head back and closes her eyes. "The dinner's at seven. I'm having a formal dinner party downstairs for a Chilean diplomat and his party. With your father away, I asked Matt to act as host. We won't be finished until late, but you'll see him at breakfast."

Suzanne pokes her head in the door. "Madam President, excuse me."

Personal secretary or no personal secretary, Suzanne knew from the beginning that Mom wanted our private rooms kept private, with no official business permitted. Mom sighs, puts on her shoes, and goes out into the hall. I'm sure that's the end of our conversation, and it is. Mom and Suzanne huddle over some papers, with Mom giving directions and Suzanne nodding a mile a minute.

I go back to my computer, but I'm still uneasy as to when Annie will get home. Okay, at the risk of her getting mad at me, I'm going to set up the dock in the wardrobe myself. Mrs. B. is due to arrive soon for the evening, so I'd better get it done before she shows up and starts asking questions.

With the new batteries installed, and the alarm set for 2 AM, I stash the dock in my backpack and peek out the door. When I see that Mom and Suzanne are both gone, I step out and head down the hall. That's the easy part.

The rest is harder. Though I try to act calm, I'm far from it. What if someone asks me where I'm going and what I'm doing? I'm breathless by the time I reach the Lincoln Bedroom. I make a quick security check. Two workmen are hanging a painting down the hall, a flower arranger is fussing with a vase of yellow tulips with her back to me, and a vacuum cleaner is whirring away in a nearby room.

I open the Lincoln Bedroom door and scoot inside.

The same dim desk light is on, but I don't allow myself to look around or think about where I am or what I'm doing. I head right for the wardrobe and open both doors, careful not to look in the mirrors. The last thing I want to see is a reflection, any reflection, including my own.

With hands that are suddenly damp, I grip the dock and the iPod tight to make sure I don't drop them. I certainly don't need to have the Gettysburg Address playing at the wrong time or not playing at all. Though it looks okay, I can only hope Annie and I put it together right.

It's too late to worry. I set the dock in the corner of the wardrobe and leave one of the doors open a couple of inches to make sure the sound carries. As I stand up, I glance in one of the wardrobe mirrors without meaning to. All I see is me, my eyes wide and looking scared. I am scared. At least if I'd waited for Annie, I'd have had company.

When I crack open the bedroom door and poke my head out, I see Suzanne down the hall talking to the flower arranger. I'll have to walk past them with my backpack, which will just lead to questions. I begin to panic. Wait, I'll hide my backpack in the bedroom and pick it up tomorrow. But where? I dart back in, look around, and make the obvious choice. I lift up the bedspread, shove the backpack under the bed, and then pull the spread down to the floor.

I wait by the door, peering down the hall. Suzanne and the flower arranger are still talking. I quickly slip out. As I pass them I smile and murmur a non-word greeting without stopping.

Annie gets home half an hour later, and instead of being mad, she's delighted when I tell her I've already hidden the dock. "That's great. You knew I didn't want to go in that room, didn't you?"

I nod as if that were my reason for taking care of everything. "Yeah, right."

Mrs. B. arrives, I go back to my computer, and Annie flops on her bed to read.

At 6:30 Chef Toni announces our dinner.

Mrs. B. has her dinner on a tray in the library, watching TV, while Annie and I eat in our alcove. To our surprise, just as we're finishing, Uncle Matt sticks his head around the corner. He's wearing a tuxedo and looks really handsome. Why did he have to show up? Seeing him makes me feel guilty about what we've planned for him, but mostly I'm still upset that he's getting to sleep in the Lincoln Bedroom and we're not.

"Hey there, kiddos." Only Uncle Matt gets away with calling us "kiddos."

Annie doesn't act guilty *or* upset. "Hi, Uncle Matt. Wow, you look handsome in your tuxedo. How come you're not at the dinner? Mom went down half an hour ago."

Uncle Matt grins. "I don't have to appear until six forty-five, and I thought I'd come up here to tell you how thrilled I am to be considered enough of a VPI—Very Privileged Individual— to sleep in the Lincoln Bedroom. My thanks, KayKay."

That's really rubbing it in. Suddenly, the apple strudel dessert that tasted delicious a few minutes ago tastes as dry as cardboard.

Uncle Matt comes over and puts his hands on my shoulders. "I'm just kidding, KayKay. And I want you to know I had a serious talk with your mother urging her to let you girls sleep there, too. I emphasized that you're both mature and responsible and she should give her permission."

That sounds more like it. "Did she say she would?"

Uncle Matt squeezes my shoulders. "Well, not exactly, but I'm sure she's thinking about it."

Annie licks her dessert plate the way she does when Mom and Dad aren't around. "It doesn't matter to me, Uncle Matt. I wouldn't sleep there anyway."

"Well, it matters to me." Actually, I'd have been surprised if Mom had changed her mind. But Uncle Matt has a lot of clout with Mom, so maybe there's hope.

Uncle Matt checks his watch. "I'd better get going."

After Uncle Matt leaves, the evening creeps by on turtle feet. Annie and I watch some TV, but it's all reruns. We consider Ping-Pong, but that takes too much effort. Dad is teaching us to play chess, but neither of us remembers how to set up the board. Finally, we turn the TV back on. At last, at nine o'clock, I give an elaborate yawn and nudge Annie to do the same. With a good-night to Mrs. B., we're off to bed.

The silent White House army has been at work, as usual. The draperies are closed, and the lights are turned off except for the lamps by our beds. The bedspreads are folded and lying on a chair, with a cozy envelope of blankets turned down just far enough to snuggle into. The presidents book that Dad gave me is on my bedside table where he left it, still not read, with Mr. Moosie and Nana on our pillows. Finding everything the way it is every night is somehow reassuring, and tonight I need reassuring.

My Mr. Moosie is a long-legged moose, while Annie's Nana is a once-white polar bear, two stuffed animals that Dad brought back from Alaska when I was two and Annie was a baby. Neither of us goes to bed without our Mr. Moosie and Nana, especially tonight.

Clutching Mr. Moosie, I look out the door to make sure no one is in the hall. I don't see anyone in either direction. Nevertheless, as I set the alarm clock I find myself whispering.

"I'm setting the alarm for one forty-five, Annie. That gives us time to get down the hall and knock on Uncle Matt's door. Borden said that Lincoln's ghost always knocks. Besides, we want to make sure Uncle Matt is wide awake by two."

Annie is already in bed, but at that, she sits up straight. "I never said I'd knock on Uncle Matt's door. What if there are no lights on in the hall? What if someone sees us? What if we get caught?"

At this point, I don't need Annie raising questions that I've already raised myself. "Nothing's going to happen. We'll knock on the door and get back here before anyone knows we're gone."

Annie lies down again, turns over, and doesn't answer.

I won't argue now. When the alarm goes off, I'll manage to get Annie to change her no to a yes the way I always do.

But when the clock buzzer sounds, I don't know where I am. It's dark, really dark. Time to get up for school? No, it's only 1:45. Then I remember. Uncle Matt! I turn on the light and pull at Annie's blanket. "Wake up. We've got to knock on Uncle Matt's door."

"I'm not going." Annie buries her face in her pillow.

Me do this alone? I don't think so. I throw back my blankets, get up, and stand over her, glowering. "Annie, you said you'd go."

"Did not."

"Did too."

Annie raises her head. "Did not."

I lean over Annie so that she'll be sure to hear me. "Remember how Uncle Matt embarrassed you when he sent you birthday flowers at school, and your class sang happy birthday to you, and it wasn't even your birthday? Now we have the perfect way to pay Uncle Matt back."

"You never said anything about knocking on his door."

Maybe I did forget to mention it, but I'm not going to tell her that. "Of course we talked about it."

"I don't care if we did. I'm not going."

I'm getting desperate. "You have to."

Annie turns over in bed and sits up. "I saw him again, that tall, skinny moving man. And no one's moving, are they? What's he doing here? Who is he? He scares me, KayKay, and I'm not going."

"You're a pathetic chicken, that's what you are," I whisper.

Silence.

I can usually get Annie to do what I want, but when she gets as stubborn as this, there's no moving her. Her problem is that she still has Dad's "undercurrent haunting the White House" on the brain. And who is this tall, skinny moving man with a beard she's always talking about? I've never even seen him.

Now I have to go down that long dark hall alone, find the right door, knock, and then get back here before anyone knows what I'm up to. If I don't do it, Uncle Matt might sleep through the whole Gettysburg Address.

I sink back down on my bed and watch the digital clock numbers flip over to 1:51 . . . 1:52. . . . It will soon be too late to wake up Uncle Matt before the Gettysburg Address plays. Mom's already bombed me out of a sleepover in the Lincoln

Bedroom, but if I don't knock on that door, I'm bombing myself out. I told myself I could pull this project off, and so far I have. I can't give up now.

I straighten my shoulders the way Mom's always nagging me to do and grab my bathrobe without even trying to be quiet. I open our bedroom door, make sure the hall is empty, and then tiptoe out.

CHAPTER EIGHT

IN WHICH A PLOT GOES AWRY

The Family Floor hall is usually lit up and filled with people. Now it's empty. A couple of low-intensity lamps are turned on, but what pale light they shed etches eerie shadows. I called Annie a pathetic chicken, but I'm not feeling all that brave myself. I should have brought a flashlight.

Nothing looks familiar as I slide my bare feet along the thick hall carpeting. Lining the walls are white marble busts with bulging eyes that stare out sightlessly, while the eyes in the portraits of long-gone people follow me. And the hallway goes on forever. Has it always been this far to the Lincoln Bedroom?

All the doors on either side of the hall are closed. After Borden told Annie and me about Abraham Lincoln's assassination, I asked Dad if any other presidents had been assassinated. I was surprised when he told me there had been three: James Garfield, William McKinley, and John Kennedy. I'd quickly looked them up in the presidents book that Dad had given me, and wished I hadn't. Nutcases shot all four presidents. I don't dare let myself start thinking that Mom might be in that kind of danger.

But what's to stop the ghosts of those other three presidents from wandering around the White House at night? Wait a minute. Dad's the one who says history haunts the White House, not me. Dad's the one who says some mysterious undercurrent keeps him awake, not me. I have a good imagination, but I'm not into ghosts and never have been. On the other hand, I made fun of Annie's tall, skinny moving man, but maybe she's on to something. I ball my hands into fists. No, I don't believe in ghosts. . . . I don't believe in ghosts. . . . I don't believe in ghosts. . . .

With my eyes straight ahead, I try not to imagine what might be behind the closed doors along the hallway. I can't help picturing the presidents who lived there, went to bed every night, got up in the morning, worked at their desks, played with their kids, all without knowing they'd be shot down some ordinary day. It makes me shiver.

There, ahead of me, I see the table with the vase of yellow tulips. The Lincoln Bedroom door just beyond it is closed, too. I raise my hand, hesitate a long moment, and then force myself to knock five times. Hard. As the five knocks echo up and down the hall, I take off at a run.

In my rush I stumble over a stool and almost trip, stub my big toe on a chair, and bump into a coffee table. I hear the clatter of something falling off, but there's no way I'm going to stop and pick it up.

By the time I reach my bedroom, I'm panting. Closing the bedroom door behind me, I take off my bathrobe and leap into bed. Reaching for Mr. Moosie, I hold him tight.

"Did you knock on Uncle Matt's door?" Annie's whisper comes from out of the dark.

I answer in gulps. "Yes—I did—no thanks—to you—" I scrunch deeper under the blankets.

"Well, so what happened?" Annie is still whispering.

I play it cool. "Nothing. I knocked five times like I planned. That's all. And by the way, I didn't run into your tall, skinny moving man."

Annie raises her voice. "You don't believe I ever saw that man, do you?"

"Well, for sure, no one else has ever seen him."

"I'm going to ask Gloria. I bet she's seen him. And you'd believe Gloria, wouldn't you?" Annie not only sounds wide awake now but also indignant.

"You ask Gloria and I'll ask Tom. If Secret Service agents haven't seen him, then he's a figment of your imagination." I love the expression "a figment of your imagination." This is the first time I've ever used it.

Annie agrees. "Asking both Gloria and Tom is fine with me. One or both of them will tell you I'm right."

It doesn't take Annie long to fall asleep, but I'm so hyped up, I'm still awake when I hear a burst of voices outside our room. Some man is talking in a foreign language. Then I hear Mom's voice say something in what sounds like the same language. It has to be Spanish. That's the only foreign language Mom knows.

I put on my bathrobe and go out into the hall.

The lights are ablaze. Mom in her robe and slippers, a short, fat, bald man in striped pajamas, and two Secret Service agents with wires running from their earpieces into their jacket collars are all talking at once. Mom looks deadly serious, while the bald man's face is red and his eyes are practically popping out. I don't know who the short, bald man is, but he's certainly super excited. He doesn't stop jabbering in Spanish for a minute. I'm beginning to get bad vibrations.

"Mom, what's going on?" I'm not sure I want to know.

Mom spins around. "Katherine, what are you doing here?"

"I heard all the noise and came out to see what's happening." No way am I going to say I was already awake. Mom knows I'm a dead-to-the-world sleeper, and she'd pump me to know why I wasn't asleep.

Mom is frowning now, a bad sign. "What's happening is that our guest, Señor Alvarez, just had a frightening experience, and we're trying to get to the bottom of it."

Uh-oh.

One of the agents is taking notes. "Do you have any idea of the time when all this happened, sir?"

Mom translates the question into what sounds like not-very-good Spanish.

The bald man answers in a torrent of words with lots of gestures.

Mom is upset by his answer, but before she can translate what he said to the agents, the door to the guest bedroom opposite Mom's sitting room opens. Uncle Matt steps out, barefoot and in his pajamas. He's putting on his bathrobe.

I gasp. It can't be Uncle Matt at this end of the hall.

But it *is* Uncle Matt. "What's up, Margaret? Is everything all right?"

Before Mom can answer, the bald man babbles more excited Spanish.

Uncle Matt nods and looks interested, as if he

understands. "Well, I'll be. What's your opinion about all this, Margaret?"

Mom shakes her head. "I can't guess, Matt. It's bizarre. Señor Alvarez says he was awakened in the Lincoln Bedroom by a pounding on the door and then a man's voice booming out from somewhere in the room. He was understandably alarmed, and so am I."

I know it's a mistake to speak up, but I have to know. "Uncle Matt, I thought you were sleeping in the Lincoln Bedroom."

Uncle Matt acts surprised to see me, as if he hadn't noticed me before. "There was a change of plans, KayKay. Señor Alvarez mentioned at dinner that he'd heard other guests had slept in the Lincoln Bedroom and he would be deeply honored if he could, too. Of course, your mother was happy to comply. So I slept here in the guest room."

Unbelievable! Of all nights, a White House guest has to show up and ask to sleep in the Lincoln Bedroom. Even worse, it's a guest that Mom was especially anxious to please. I remember her telling Suzanne she didn't want any hitches.

I'd call this a major hitch, and it's a sure thing Mom does, too.

Uncle Matt says something to Señor Alvarez in Spanish before turning back to Mom. "Can I help with the translating, Margaret?"

Mom shakes her head. "No thanks, Matt. Dennis and Ralph here have everything under control."

My expression probably looks as thunderstruck as I feel, and I don't want Mom to notice. Hoping no one will stop me, I ease my way backward into my room, quietly close the door, and slip into bed . . . but not to sleep.

CHAPTER NINE

IN WHICH THE CULPRITS ARE PUNISHED

In her robe and slippers Mom marches into Annie's and my bedroom Sunday morning looking for bear. Mom never loses her temper. She doesn't need to. Her frown lines do that for her. When we see that frown, we know she's angry, and her frown level this morning is awesome.

I don't fool Mom for a minute. "That was quite a stunt you pulled last night, Katherine. I won't bore you with the details, but Dennis and Ralph found your iPod in the wardrobe, not to mention your backpack under the bed. And they had no trouble tracking down how you and Ann bought a CD of the Gettysburg Address in the Visitor Center."

Annie's awake now and looking from Mom to me. Even half-asleep she senses something has gone seriously wrong. At least she has the sense to keep her mouth shut. But Mom is clearly expecting a response from me.

"I'm really sorry, Mom. It was meant to be a joke on Uncle Matt."

Mom tightens the sash on her robe as if girding for battle. "Well, I don't hear anyone laughing, do you? First off, both of you are to apologize to Señor Alvarez as soon as he finishes breakfast. Then I want you two to come to my West Wing office for a chat after we get back from church."

Seeing how upset Mom is makes me feel bad. I know she has enough on her mind without Annie and me messing up and getting some guest from Chile all hysterical. But . . . but . . . she probably doesn't realize we never would have done it if she'd let us sleep in the Lincoln Bedroom. Still, does Mom think about what's important to Annie and me anyway? No, she doesn't. But that's not fair, either. She's the greatest, and once she gets used to being president, she'll go back to being more of a mom-mom, the way she used to be—I hope.

While Mom has breakfast with Señor Alvarez, Uncle Matt, Annie, and I eat in the alcove. Uncle Matt can't stop smiling. "Thought you'd pull off a trick on your old uncle Matt, did you?" He laughs. "Actually, I congratulate you on your ingenuity. It was a whale of an idea. Put that kind of effort into your schoolwork and you'll both sail into Harvard."

Uncle Matt thinks it's all very funny, but Annie and I aren't in a laughing mood. Mom's "chats" are reserved for serious offenses. And I can kiss good-bye to any possibility that we'll ever be allowed to sleep in the Lincoln Bedroom.

As for Señor Alvarez, how hard can it be to apologize to someone who doesn't speak English? To our surprise, Señor Alvarez speaks English very well and he couldn't be nicer. He tells Annie and me that he was so excited in the night that all he could come up with was Spanish. And he's sure his eleven-year-old son will get a good laugh out of his papa running around the White House in his pajamas at two o'clock in the morning. Señor Alvarez gives both of us a farewell handshake.

After church we start out on our "last mile" walk to the West Wing. We take our time and walk slowly past the Rose Garden, along the outdoor colonnade that connects the White House and the West Wing. In the summertime the Rose Garden probably looks great, but today is cold and rainy, with not a rose in sight.

I don't want to give Annie the idea I believe in her ghost, but I'm curious. "Well, what do you think, Annie, does Señor Alvarez look like that moving man you're always talking about?"

Annie gives a snort. "Of course not. The moving man is bald like Señor Alvarez, but he's tall and skinny, not short and fat."

So much for getting anywhere with tracking Annie's mystery man.

Even on a Sunday the West Wing outer office is humming. Two women are at computers, an intern is using the copier, and Mrs. Morgan, Mom's gray-haired, Number One presidential secretary, is talking to her assistant.

If someone asked me to describe the White House, I'd say it's a giant beehive buzzing with busy bees guarding, cleaning, repairing, painting, changing lightbulbs, moving furniture, arranging flowers, or glued to their cell phones. And we're supposed to be pleasant to all of them. Right now, when Annie and I are about to face the queen bee, I'd just as soon not have to be pleasant to anyone.

But Annie and I are greeted with smiles. I try to smile back, but my mind is on the Oval Office and Mom twenty feet away. Mrs. Morgan gets up from her desk and knocks on the Oval Office door.

"Katherine and Ann are here, Madam President."

Mrs. Morgan waves us in. The few times I've been in the West Wing, I've noticed visitors waiting to see Mom are nervous. I'm nervous, too, but then why wouldn't I be? The Oval Office is pretty overwhelming.

Mom is at her desk, the presidential flag with an eagle holding an olive branch in one talon and arrows in the other is to her left, with the

American flag on her right. Another presidential seal is woven into the center of the dark blue rug. Even Mom's massive desk is impressive. Mom told us that Great Britain's Queen Victoria gave the desk to one of our presidents more than a hundred years ago, and almost every president since then has used it.

Mom is frowning as she waves Annie and me into two stiff-backed chairs. "I have a busy morning, so I'll be brief. Katherine and Ann, I can't tell you how disappointed I am in both of you, especially you, Katherine, as it doesn't take much imagination to know you were the instigator."

I squirm. "Yes, but Uncle Matt was supposed to sleep in—"

Mom interrupts. "I know it's not easy having the spotlight constantly on you, and I don't want either of you to be cowed by it. Nevertheless, the White House entails special privileges and demands certain behavior in return. The White House doesn't belong to us Grangers or to any president. A guest in the White House is a guest of the country, whether the guest is Señor Alvarez or your uncle Matt. Every guest should be treated with respect and consideration, neither of which you displayed last night. The situation in Chile is politically sensitive right now, and Señor Alvarez's experience wasn't the least bit helpful."

Mom pauses as she looks down at a list on her desk. A list? That's not good. I press our case. "Uncle Matt's always playing tricks on us, Mom. We were just trying to pay him back. He thought it was funny."

Mom looks unconvinced. "I know he did, and he urged me to go easy on you. However, since your father isn't here to talk this over with, I have to do what I think best. You're both grounded for two weeks. You're to watch no television. You'll use your computers strictly for homework. You're to come straight home from school. You'll take over Harris's job of setting and clearing the dinner table. And the lunch-and-movie day with your friends is off."

"Oh no!" This is worse than I expected.

Annie is upset, too. "Mom, please let us have the Granger Film Festival."

Annie and I were to have each invited a friend for a Saturday lunch and a showing of two new movies that aren't out yet. I latched onto the title Granger Film Festival hoping it would become a tradition.

"No, Ann. I'm sorry, but that's final." Mom starts shuffling papers again to indicate our "chat" is finished.

And that is that.

For once Suzanne does us a favor. She hasn't ordered the movies yet, so Annie and I haven't invited anyone, which means we don't have to do any disinviting. I was planning to invite Alix, a really friendly girl I admire a lot who has the locker next to mine, while Annie was going to have Meghan, her ice-skating buddy.

For the rest of Sunday, my mood matches the weather, dreary and depressing.

My Monday mood isn't much better. Instead of bragging to Borden at lunch about our triumph with Uncle Matt, I tell him about what I've come to call the Chile Disaster. "So that's it. Annie and I are grounded for two weeks."

While I'm talking, Borden is looking soulfully at my double-chocolate brownie. He grins as I split it and hand over half.

"Thanks." He takes a bite. "Personally, I don't see what the big deal is. Teddy Roosevelt's kids jumped out of potted palms to scare guests. They roller-skated in the East Room, took a pony upstairs in the elevator, and everyone thought they were cute." Borden polishes off his brownie. "Hey, how about you and me bowling a few frames this afternoon? I'll give you some pointers."

Although I'm not into bowling pointers, I've begun to see another side to Borden. Maybe when our grounding is up, I'll listen to his bowling pointers if he agrees to listen to my creative writing pointers. "Sorry about that, Borden, but no one thought we were cute. We're both out of commission for two weeks."

When the next-period buzzer sounds, Borden and I part company. Borden has band, and I head for my locker to pick up my social studies assignment.

Alix is opening her locker next to mine. "I can't believe you're having lunch practically every day with The Borden, KayKay. Are you crazy?"

I'm so surprised, I don't respond.

She isn't finished anyway. "What a world-class

geek. Keep on doing that and you are *so* socially dead."

I can't believe it. Alix is always friendly with everyone, all smiles and giggles.

"Borden's not so bad," I say. "He can be really funny."

Alix stops combing her hair long enough to stick her head around my locker door. "Yeah, he's funny, all right, if you mean weird funny."

What happened to the I-love-everyone Alix? I'm beginning not to like this. "I don't mean weird funny. I mean ha-ha funny. You just don't know Borden."

Alix slams her locker shut. "And don't want to. Well, each to his own, as they say."

As I race down the hall to social studies class I remember that when Borden came to the White House with his grandparents, I was as negative as Alix. But look how helpful he's been all this past week. And nice. Maybe he has to brag and talk all the time because he doesn't feel that great about himself.

As for Alix, now that I think about it, her smiles and giggling are only with the in-kids. She didn't get smiley and giggly with me until Mom became president. If I keep having lunch with Borden, she'll probably drop me so I don't contaminate her. I instantly decide that if Annie and I ever have a Granger Film Festival, Alix is out and Borden is in.

Mrs. B. is on duty when we get home that afternoon. I can hardly wait for Dad to come back from San Francisco so that we don't have to have Mrs. B. baby-sit.

Finally, on Friday afternoon Dad's waiting by the elevator as Annie and I get home from school.

But Mom has been waiting for Dad to come home, too. She's made a six o'clock appointment that night to see Dad, Annie, and me in her sitting room. Annie and I know all too well what this is about. We perch on the sofa by the window to get as far away from the action as possible.

Mom has cooled down since our West Wing "chat." At least she isn't frowning, though she isn't smiling, either. As for Dad, he cocks his head to one side as Mom tells him about the Chile Disaster. He gives a little chuckle, starts to comment, and then stops.

"I'm sorry, girls," is all he says. I don't know if that means he's sorry we did something wrong, sorry our plan backfired, sorry that we're being punished, or all three. I just bet he thinks our punishment is too stiff, but from past experience I know he'll support Mom. And he does.

We don't see much of Mom for the next ten days. She makes two quick trips on Air Force One, first to Chicago and then to the West Coast. Maybe it's wishful thinking to count on Mom ever being around more. At least when she's here, she doesn't act mad, or if she is, she doesn't show it. She treats us just like she always has lately, that is, pleasant but distant.

While she's away, Dad and Mrs. B. take up the slack. Dad is still trying to teach Annie and me how to play chess. It's like math, only interesting, and maybe learning how each move leads to the next move will help me solve algebra problems, step-by-step. When Dad isn't around, Mrs. B. takes over. She's determined to teach Annie and me to knit. We give it a try but find out fast that knitting is one tiny stitch at a time with everything measured in mini-inches.

Chef Toni pitches in, too. She arrives on Sunday morning to show me how to make bread. And she's given me hope. She says she's always been small, too, but she kneads dough like a sumo wrestler. As for me, my arms ache after a few minutes. Though kneading the dough, letting it rise, then kneading it again takes hours, when I smell the bread baking, it's worth the effort.

During those ten days I miss a school play and Annie misses a birthday party sleepover. But Annie's allowed to take her skating lessons, and I put in time writing my mystery.

The countess's jewels aren't stolen after all. She and her ski-instructor boyfriend have hidden her jewels in an abandoned miner's shack on the mountain. She then reports the jewels stolen to collect the insurance. Madison and Lori are caught in a blizzard while skiing and take refuge in the shack, where they find the jewels. The ski instructor traps them in the shack, ties them up, and leaves them to freeze. A helicopter, flown by Sean Cooper (alias Uncle Matt), comes to their rescue, after which Madison helps the police identify and arrest the culprits. The End.

Being grounded for two weeks gave me the idea of having Madison and Lori helpless and tied up in a shack. As far as I can see, being grounded isn't much different. It seems like forever before parole time rolls around. Annie and I can hardly wait to get home from school on our last day.

Suzanne stops us on our way to our bedroom. "Your mother wants to see you at six o'clock this evening in her sitting room." Her lips are a thin, tight line, as if she knows all about the Chile Disaster and disapproves. Having the countess in my mystery look and act like Suzanne gives me special pleasure.

When Annie and I come into Mom's sitting room at six, she's on the phone. After she finishes, she gives us her real-life smile, not her political it's-nice-to-meet-you smile. It's a wonderful smile that brings out dimples that don't show any other time. "Well, well, here you are. Congratulations! I'm so proud of you two. You've taken your punishment like troopers. Best of all, I never heard a word of complaint from either of you."

Of course Mom hasn't heard any complaints. Dad has, Mrs. B. has, our friends at school have, but we made sure Mom hasn't.

I smile. "Thanks, Mom."

"Yeah, thanks, Mom," Annie echoes.

Mom stands up as if she's about to make a great pronouncement. And she is. "Your penalties are over. Furthermore, your father and I talked last night and agreed that as a reward for your mature attitude, the two of you can spend this coming Friday night in the Lincoln Bedroom."

The Lincoln Bedroom! After the Chile Disaster, I was sure that Annie and I would never get to sleep in the Lincoln Bedroom. Now Mom's changed her mind. I read somewhere that changing your mind is the sign of a big person. That's Mom, all right.

But Annie looks stricken.

I have to get her on board. "Hey, Annie, it'll be the best. That's a huge bed in there. We'll have Nana and Mr. Moosie with us. We can leave a light on and—"

A knock on the door interrupts me. It's Suzanne with mail and a big box. "This package was just delivered from Lombardo's, Madam President. I know you've been waiting for it. And I picked up your personal mail."

"Thanks, Suzanne. Please put the package in

my bedroom." Suzanne hands the mail to Mom and then leaves with the box. Glancing through the mail, Mom holds up a postcard. "Look, girls, here's a card from your uncle Matt in Stockholm. What a beautiful city. Someday the four of us will go to Sweden."

I'm more interested in the box. Mom and Dad are invited to a French Embassy reception in Mom's honor, and her gown was designed by a famous designer. "Mom, is that your new dress in the box? Can we see it?"

"Not now, Katherine. I'm anxious to finish these phone calls. I'll tell you what, though, you and Annie can stay up Friday night to see your dad and me in all our finery before you get settled in the Lincoln Bedroom."

Mom has never been much of a hugger, but before Annie and I leave, she gives each of us a hug before she sits down and reaches for her phone.

A hug from Mom is a treat. Maybe she's feeling guilty she's been so tough on Annie and me. I lean over and give Mom a big hug back.

CHAPTER TEN

IN WHICH AN ALLY
IS ENLISTED

I'm not going to tell Borden that I'll be sleeping in the Lincoln Bedroom this coming Friday night. I want to surprise him. After the big event I plan to cook up a terrifying story about Annie and me facing down Lincoln's ghost.

But by Thursday I'm too excited to keep it a secret, and I blurt out the news.

Borden's eyes light up behind his glasses. "Hey, with this being Presidents' Day weekend, it's perfect timing. Actually, Lincoln was born on February 12, 1809, and Washington on February 11, 1731. But in 1752, the old calendar was changed to the calendar we use now, so that the new year began on January first instead of March twenty-fifth, and the calendar was jumped ahead by eleven days. That made George Washington's birthdate fall officially on February 22, 1732."

Probably Borden knows so much, he can't help sounding like an encyclopedia. I have no idea what he's talking about. I'm thankful I'm not that smart, though a little smarter wouldn't be bad.

To everyone's surprise, including the weathermen who forecasted snow showers, a blizzard blows in. Great! The storm will give me firsthand research on what a blizzard is like when Madison and Lori are trapped on the mountain in my mystery.

It snows all Thursday afternoon, Thursday night, and into Friday. On Friday every school in Washington is closed. Annie was to have been a finalist in a metro-Washington spelling bee Friday afternoon. She was all psyched up, so while everyone else is cheering that schools will be closed on Friday, as well as Monday for Presidents' Day, she's totally frustrated.

Mom couldn't have gone to the spelling bee anyway. She'd already explained to Annie that she has a meeting that she can't change. At least Dad and I were geared up to sit front row center and cheer Annie on. So far, the media hasn't gotten wind of Annie being a finalist, which pleases her as much as being a contestant.

Right now Annie is still insisting she won't sleep in the Lincoln Bedroom tonight, and I'm still trying to talk her into it. Though I'm not concerned about the possibility of a ghost sighting—absolutely not—I'd really like company in that huge bed.

Annie doesn't have a clue I want to sleep there for research, and I'm not going to tell her. It's my golden opportunity to learn what mysteries are all about—how to sort out the elements of a mystery and how to weave them into a story. And I don't need Annie giving me a hard time about writing a mystery, like she did when she snuck into my computer. I don't need her calling me Nancy Drew again, either.

A no-school day gives me a chance to work on Annie. I launch my campaign at breakfast. "Count on getting years of credit with teachers for sleeping in the Lincoln Bedroom, Annie. And think how jealous Uncle Matt will be when he finds out we slept in the Lincoln Bedroom and he didn't."

Annie doesn't take the bait. "I told you, I'm not going to do it. This is Presidents' Day weekend. Abraham Lincoln could show up for his birthday."

That possibility crossed my mind, too, though I'd never admit it to Annie. "C'mon, you know Lincoln's birthday was ten days ago. Presidents' Day weekend is no big deal. It was only dreamed up to give everyone a three-day holiday."

Annie's not convinced. I'll have to bring out my big guns. "All right, Annie, if you want to sleep in your own bed, that's fine. But I won't be there, Mom and Dad will be gone all night at their party, and Mom told me Mrs. B. will be staying available for us in the Lincoln Sitting Room. You'll be down at this end of the hall all alone."

Annie eyes widen. "You're kidding!"

I see light at the end of the tunnel. "No, I'm not kidding, but don't worry, you'll be safe. I'll check to make sure all the windows are locked. Then you can lock the bedroom door and put something heavy like a table or chair up against it."

Annie's eyes are wide open. "What if I lock myself in and can't get out?"

I press on. "There'll be plenty of people around in the morning who can get you out."

Annie blinks as if she's close to tears. "This isn't good."

Aha, she's breaking. "And you've got your cell phone in case you need to call for help."

Annie's silent for a long moment, and I know I have her. "If I sleep with you in the Lincoln Bedroom will you leave a light on all night?" Her voice is husky.

I've got her!

"Definitely."

"Can we have Nana and Mr. Moosie with us?"

"Of course."

"And Mrs. B. will really be there?"

"Right next door in the Lincoln Sitting Room."

"Well, okay . . . I guess."

That's it. I won't have to spend the night alone.

With the Lincoln Bedroom on both our minds, the day drags. I try to work on my mystery, but Annie is so itchy, she keeps interrupting me until

I give up. I'm almost ready to resort to doing home-work when the snow stops, and Annie and I go sledding down the South Lawn. Mom used to sled with us in our old life but hasn't for a couple of years.

Instead, Tom and Gloria stand on duty, stamp-ing their feet and rubbing their hands to keep warm. While we were getting the sleds out, Annie gave them a description of her moving man. No, neither one had seen anyone who looked like that. Figment of Annie's imagination, that's what he is.

After dinner in the kitchen alcove, Annie and I turn on the TV but we're too excited to pay much attention. In the end we get ready for bed early and then play a couple of computer games. At nine o'clock Annie with Nana and me with Mr. Moosie head down the hall in our bathrobes to watch Mom and Dad get ready for the French Embassy party.

We settle down on Mom's chaise lounge for the fashion show. Mom, who is tall and stately with perfect posture, stands with her shoulders back, the way she's always nagging me to stand. Janelle, her hairstylist, has done her hair in a todie-for French braid, and her beautiful blue-green designer gown that matches her eyes sparkles with crystal beading.

Like me, Annie is entranced. "Mom, you look beautiful, more like a queen than a president."

Mom laughs, but she's obviously pleased.

Dad, who is struggling with his white tie, finally gives up and lets Mom tie it. "How about me, girls, am I beautiful, too, like a beautiful penguin?"

Dad will never be tall and stately, and truthfully, with his white tie and tails he does look a little like a penguin. But I'm as proud of him as I am of Mom. Though he's known as the husband of the president, it doesn't bother him. Maybe that's because he loves Mom a lot. And he's kept his sense of humor.

With her gown swishing at every step, Mom takes Dad's arm and they walk Annie and me to the Lincoln Sitting Room. The sitting room's gold and blue furniture looks cozy and practical, not like the stiff, ugly furniture in the Lincoln Bedroom next door. Mrs. B., who is seated in a big, overstuffed chair knitting, stands as soon as she sees Mom, the way everyone does. She's her usual chirpy self. "Good evening, good evening. And my, doesn't everyone look handsome."

Annie seems comforted by the sight of grandmotherly Mrs. B. knitting away. She kisses Mom and Dad good-night and goes in. Instead of listening to one of Mrs. B.'s cheery monologues, I escort Mom and Dad to the elevator.

Mom's agent, Caitlin, and Dad's agent, Ryan, are waiting. Caitlin is elegant in a slinky black dress with spaghetti straps. Ryan is in white tie and tails, like Dad.

Of course, Mom has everything organized. "Mrs. Bruning will get you two settled, Katherine, and then she'll be next door in the Lincoln Sitting Room if you need anything. We'll be back sometime around two."

Dad groans. "I bet the midnight supper won't even be served until two. I should have gotten something to eat with the girls to keep me going."

The elevator door opens. Mom gives me a quick kiss, and then she and Caitlin step in, their skirts rustling.

Dad hesitates. "You're sure you and Annie will be all right, KayKay?"

I've made such a big deal of wanting to sleep in the Lincoln Bedroom that I can't announce now that I'm having second thoughts. Annie will be counting on me to get her through the night, but who's going to get me through the night? And I've done something dumb. Once Mom and Dad are gone, I'll have to walk back through the half-lit hall past all those closed doors and blank-eyed busts.

I force a smile. "I'm fine. And Dad, I meant to tell you that I looked up Abraham Lincoln in the book you gave me so I'd be ready for tonight. It says he only went to one full year of school his whole life. He was such a good writer, I couldn't believe it. And his mother died when he was nine. . . ." I babble on to postpone their leaving.

Dad gives me a hug. "I have to go, KayKay. Your mother is waiting. We'll see you in the morning. Love you."

I return Dad's hug with an extra-hard hug back. "Love you, Dad. Love you, too, Mom. Have fun."

From the elevator Mom blows me a kiss and gives her half-wave, half-salute good-bye as Dad and Ryan join her. The door closes.

The hum of the elevator fades. They're gone. I'm alone, alone for that walk back to the Lincoln Bedroom. The outdoor spotlights shining in the big east window at the far end of the hall throw hide-and-seek shadows on the ceiling. I bite my lip to summon up courage.

I turn to head back. And then it happens, my worst nightmare come to life. The door opposite the elevator opens and a man steps out into the hall holding something in his hand.

I freeze, unable even to scream.

CHAPTER ELEVEN

IN WHICH A NIGHT'S SLEEP IS INTERRUPTED

I can only stare at the man as he walks toward me. I go weak with relief when I realize what he's holding in his hand is only a cell phone. But I still can't speak.

He must see how paralyzed I am. "Hey, I'm sorry I startled you. I guess you weren't told that I'll be on duty with you and your sister tonight at the Lincoln Bedroom. I'm Agent Robert Todd."

It takes a moment to put together what he's saying. But now that he's under one of the dimmed hall chandeliers, I see he has an earpiece in his ear and a wire running into his collar. And he's wearing a business suit and striped tie like all the agents wear. Are these Secret Service people trained to be stealthy? They could scare the wits out of a statue.

Now that the first shock has passed, my breathing begins to return to normal, and I get a closer look at Robert Todd. He's medium tall and pudgy, with a mustache and slicked-down dark hair. Since I've never seen him on the Family Floor, he must have been assigned to Annie and me from some other duty. At least he isn't tall and skinny with a beard like Annie's moving man.

As we start down the hall I can't help focusing on the night ahead. "About Abraham Lincoln . . . everyone says his ghost haunts the White House?" I give a little laugh and let the sentence drift off into a question, as if I personally would never believe anything so ridiculous.

Robert laughs, too. "I can't imagine Abraham Lincoln as a ghost. Abraham Lincoln was a loving family man who was crazy about his boys. Why, Tad and Willie got into outrageous mischief, and Pa never scolded them. He was much too soft-hearted ever to go around frightening people."

"Oh, it's not me who worries about that kind

of stuff, it's my sister." Though I'm certainly not expecting to see Abraham Lincoln's ghost, I'm glad Robert reassured me. He's so convincing, I'm sorry Annie wasn't here, too.

Robert opens the Lincoln Bedroom door. "I'll be right here in the hall all night. See you in the morning." He steps back to let me in and then closes the door behind me.

To my surprise the room is lit up, but empty. Annie and Mrs. B. must still be in the Sitting Room. Then I notice that the rocking chair with its back to me is going back and forth. Someone is in the rocking chair! Abraham Lincoln was sitting in a rocking chair when he was shot at Ford's Theater. He's here now—in his rocking chair!

I can't move or even cry out. And then the rocking stops, and a figure stands up. I make a gargling sound that's half a sob and half a laugh. It's Mrs. B.

But if Mrs. B. is here, where is Annie?

Mrs. B. answers my question before I ask it. "Ann's in the bathroom, dear. She'll be right out. And here you are, all ready for bed. What my grandson wouldn't give to be in your place. He reads everything he can about Lincoln and the Civil War. You two are lucky, lucky girls."

After my scare by the elevator, and my panic at the sight of the back-and-forth rocking chair, I'm not sure I agree with her. Annie doesn't, either. She comes through the Sitting Room door just in time to hear the "lucky, lucky girls" comment and makes a face behind Mrs. B.'s back.

Neither of us says anything as Mrs. B. takes the bedspread off the bed. "Suzanne asked me to tell you to be extra careful with this coverlet. One of our First Ladies crocheted it almost a hundred years ago when her husband was president."

Does Suzanne think we're going to knot up the spread and use it to escape out a window? I wonder why anyone would make it in the first place. Mom certainly wouldn't, but then Mom doesn't even sew on buttons. Dad, who learned to sew in the Navy, is our family stitcher-upper.

Mrs. B. folds the spread, lays it over a chair, and then makes sure the draperies are closed. "I see you girls brought your teddy bears. I had a teddy bear once. I just loved him to death. His name was Lou Willie Bear."

Annie is insulted. She holds up Nana. "Nana

isn't a teddy bear, Mrs. B. Nana is a nickname for Nanuk, which is Inuit for polar bear, and that's what he is. And Mr. Moosie isn't a teddy bear, either. He's called Mr. Moosie because he's a moose."

Mrs. B. is only half listening. "That's nice, Ann. Now you two hop in bed. It's late. I'll be right next door in the Sitting Room. Oh yes, and your mother asked me to leave a light on for you."

Mrs. B. turns off all the lights but the one on the desk. "I guess that's it. Well, good night, Katherine. Good night, Ann. Sleep tight." As Mrs. B. goes into the Sitting Room she shuts the door between the two rooms.

We climb into the mammoth bed with its carved headboard reaching almost to the ceiling. The bed looks lumpy, but to my surprise it's really comfortable. But my feet reach only halfway down, and even with Annie next to me, I can stretch my arms out. I'm perfectly still, my eyes open. I know Annie's awake, too. She gives a little sniff between each breath.

It's amazing to realize I'm finally here, lying in the bed where Abraham Lincoln once slept. If Abraham Lincoln did sleep, he did better than me. I'm so wide awake, I don't think I'll ever fall asleep.

As my eyes adjust to the faint light from the desk I glance around the room. Borden called the furniture old-fashioned. I call it weird. The sofa in the corner looks more like a figure crouched over, ready to spring, and that table with the four stork legs is the ugliest table I've ever seen. As for the ticking antique clock on the mantelpiece, I'm used to silent digital clocks with numbers that light up. I'd never get used to a clock that ticks like the beat of a living heart.

The windows are all closed, but the draperies stir ever so slightly. Maybe those hideous, long-beaked storks are hiding behind the draperies, their beady eyes peering out at us. That image does it. I turn on the bedside light, swing my feet onto the floor, and stand up. Though I hoped sleeping here would get me into the heart of writing a mystery, I had no idea my imagination would get so out of control. To imagine those carved birds hiding behind the draperies is as dumb as Annie's obsession with her moving-man ghost.

Annie's imagination is working overtime, too. "Check and see if there's anything in the wardrobe." Her voice is a croaky whisper.

I tiptoe over to the wardrobe. Making sure not to look in either mirror, I pull on the doors, but they stick. From inside the wardrobe I hear a rattle that stops me dead.

Annie's voice is muffled. "What's that noise?"

Without answering, I hold my breath, grip the doors, and pull hard to open them. The wardrobe is empty except for four or five rattling hangers. Hangers!

"It's nothing, just hangers." I hope Annie doesn't notice my voice is shaky.

She doesn't. She's already on to her next worry. "What if we need help? There's no phone."

I've already noticed that. I should have brought my cell phone. I try to sound unconcerned. "Hey, what's to get excited about? Mrs. B. is right next door, and Robert's in the hall."

"Who's Robert?"

"Robert Todd, an agent. He's on duty out there all night."

Annie props herself up on her elbows. "I didn't

see anyone in the hall when I went to the bathroom."

"He just arrived. We met at the elevator and he walked me back here. To make you happy, though, I'll check to make sure he's still there, and then I'll lock our door."

Robert's in the hall, all right. He's leaning against the wall cleaning his fingernails. When he sees me, he gives a thumbs-up signal.

Cleaning fingernails is such an ordinary thing to do, I feel better. I wave back and close the door. "See, I told you, Annie. Robert's right there."

But when I go to lock the door, there's no lock. I jiggle the knob a couple of times so that Annie will think I'm locking up. That leaves one more thing to do before I get back in bed. Those wardrobe mirrors where Borden says he saw Lincoln's face get to me.

What about the folded bedspread on the chair? It would make a perfect cover. When I open the spread, I see GRACE COOLIDGE in fancy letters across the top. She must have been the president's wife who made it. I toss the spread carefully over the mirrors and straighten it out so that both mirrors are hidden. Thanks, Grace.

That does it. I don't care what Annie wants or doesn't want. I refuse to check under the bed or behind the draperies. All I care about is getting into bed with Mr. Moosie. But as I head for bed I notice the miniature statue of Abraham Lincoln on the table. He's so lifelike that I can just picture him standing up and making his way across the room on tiny feet to *his* bed. I have to get there first. I run the last few steps, jump into bed, reach for Mr. Moosie. And panic.

Mr. Moosie is gone. I feel all around my feet and under my pillow. No Mr. Moosie. He's been spirited away. Annie's just lying there. How could she let this happen? Wait a minute, there he is on the floor. He must have fallen out of bed when I got up. I hang over the side, grab him, and snuggle down under the blankets as far as I can go.

Annie is still wide awake. "What time is it?"

I have to squint to see the numbers on the mantelpiece clock. "Ten after ten."

My bedside lamp shines right in my eyes. I turn it off. I don't fall asleep for a long time, but finally the ticking of the clock lulls me into a dopey kind of trance. How long I'm out I have no idea, but all of a sudden, I wake up with a jerk.

Next to me Annie mumbles something and turns over.

Then it hits me like a kick to the stomach. A knock on the door was what woke me. A knock! Abraham Lincoln always knocks. . . .

"Mrs. B.! Mrs. B.!" I yell.

Instantly awake, Annie sits bolt upright. "What is it? What happened?"

And then she hears it, too, another loud knock on the door. "You're—you're sure the door is locked?"

I don't answer. "Mrs. B.! Mrs. B.!" The Secret Service agent. What's his name? Robert. "Robert, hurry! Come quick!"

And then there's one last knock. Every thought flees as the door creaks open. Annie dives under the covers, but my eyes are riveted on the door. The desk lamp lights up a tall, thin fig-ure standing in the doorway. The figure wears a black frock coat, a shawl draped around the shoulders, and a tall stovepipe hat.

CHAPTER TWELVE

IN WHICH THE TABLES ARE TURNED

My eyes are locked on the figure standing in the doorway. At least the brim of the stovepipe hat and the shawl wrapped up high shadow his face. The last thing I want is to see his face . . . or eyes. Abraham Lincoln! It can't be, and yet it is. There is no such thing as ghosts. Yet here he is. And then the figure raises his arm and beckons to me.

With that terrifying gesture, I disconnect. Part of me hovers safely up by the ceiling looking down on the other me lying still as stone in bed. I pooh-poohed Dad's ghosts in the White House. Now Abraham Lincoln has knocked to come in, and stands in the doorway beckoning to Annie and me.

"It's you—I'm sorry we're here—in your room—in your bed—" As if from a great distance, I hear my voice, though I haven't made a decision to speak. "I live here in the White House with my family—my sister and I—we're having a sleepover—" That voice from the bed is babbling on. A sleepover. What a dumb thing to say to Abraham Lincoln.

He doesn't react. He just stands there. Maybe he's angry we're in his bed. If he comes in, what should we do? If we try to escape, where can we go?

From under the covers Annie gives a whimper. Annie's whimper snaps me back. I got us into this. I have to get us out. But how? No one answered my call for help. Where is Robert? Where is Mrs. B.?

Maybe Abraham Lincoln showed up in the Sitting Room first and Mrs. B. dropped dead of a heart attack. I think I'm having a heart attack myself. My heart is thudding like it's trying to get out of my chest.

Annie's feeble little voice comes from under the covers. "Is he still there?"

Before I can answer, Abraham Lincoln gives an odd kind of wave and backs off into the hall. Gone, he's gone! Hold it. What thought processes I still have are zeroing in on something. It's like trying to remember someone's name that stays just out of reach. The something at the back of my mind is just out of reach, too.

"I can't look. Is he there?" Annie's voice is still a croaky whisper.

"No."

The memory of that final wave has finally clicked my thinking out of STOP and into GO. My heart begins to settle down, and my breathing eases. I pause, working through everything in my head as if I were trying to picture how a new recipe will turn out. As I run down exactly what Abraham Lincoln did and how he did it, the answer jumps out at me. In one quick motion I throw back the blankets and roll out of bed.

Annie pokes her head out from under the covers. "What are you doing?"

I hold my hand up. "Stay here."

Annie clutches Nana. "What do you mean? Where are you going?"

"I'm going to find Mr. Lincoln."

Annie leaps out of bed, too. "Don't leave me! You can't leave me!"

As soon as I reach the bedroom door, I look for Robert. He's nowhere in sight. Some agent! I yank the Lincoln Sitting Room door open. The lights are still on, but Mrs. B. is gone, knitting and all. For a second I panic again. Maybe something has happened to Robert and Mrs. B.

No, of course it hasn't. Abraham Lincoln wouldn't harm either one of them, I'm sure of it. I step into the hall. The big window to my right looks out on a black, starless night sky. I look left and see Abraham Lincoln, his back to me, walking away. I start after him. But I don't hurry. I need time to decide how I'll handle this.

"Stop . . . wait . . . I'm coming." Annie catches up to me, breathless and clutching Nana.

Annie sticks right behind me as I weave around chairs, tables, and busts in the dim light. And there up ahead, the tall, thin figure is striding ahead of me. Stately is a good word to describe that walk.

I call out. "Stop, Abraham Lincoln. Stop!"

Abraham Lincoln hesitates a moment and then keeps going. I've almost caught up to him when I crash into a table, hitting my shin so hard that I cry out. With that, Abraham Lincoln stops. But instead of turning around, he bows his head and his shoulders shake as if he were crying. I remember Borden describing Lincoln's dream. "The president—" the soldier told Lincoln—". . . killed by an assassin." I'd cry, too, if I had that dream.

Maybe I'm wrong. Like Dad and Borden say, this is the White House. Anything could happen here, maybe even Abraham Lincoln haunting the halls at night. After all, plenty of people say they've seen him.

No, I'm positive I'm right. I walk toward the tall, bent figure. I step around him so that the two of us are face-to-face. I guessed that Abraham Lincoln wasn't crying, and he isn't. He's laughing.

I feel a surge of triumph. "So it *is* you."

"KayKay, what are you doing? Come back." It's Annie. She's standing a good ten feet behind me, a horrified look on her face.

I wave her on. "Come here, Annie. I want to show you something."

Annie doesn't answer. She just shakes her head.

I try to reassure her. "Don't worry, everything's fine."

Annie shakes her head even more emphatically.

I walk back and take her arm. "I have a surprise for you."

But Annie resists, so that I almost have to pull her to where Abraham Lincoln stands waiting, his back still to us.

Then Abraham Lincoln takes off his stovepipe hat and turns around. I laugh. "Take a look at what we have here, Annie."

Annie's mouth literally drops open. "Mom, it's you? I don't believe it!"

My shin hurts, and I rub it. "Believe it. Abraham Lincoln is Mom, or I should say Mom is Abraham Lincoln."

Annie is furious. "Mom, how could you do that? I was scared to death."

Mom leans down and gives Annie a hug that includes Nana, too. "I thought you two would know right away it was me and have a good laugh."

Annie stamps her foot. "Laugh? I thought you were Abraham Lincoln's ghost."

Mom looks concerned. "I didn't know you'd take me so seriously. I'm sorry, girls. I really am."

Why would Mom think we'd figure it was a joke when it's been so long since she's kidded around or had fun with us? But I'm not going to tell her that. And I'm not going to tell her how panicked I was, either. Or how I almost brain-washed myself into believing that Lincoln's ghost *does* haunt the White House. Instead, like Annie, I'm getting angry. "How could we know it was you with your face all covered up?"

Behind Mom I see Dad hurrying down the hall, still in his white tie and tails. "Ah, here you are. So what did you girls think of your visit from Mr. Lincoln?"

So Dad was in on this, too.

Mom doesn't give Annie or me a chance to answer. "Not much, I'm afraid. I frightened the girls out of a year's growth. I waited for them to recognize me, but when they didn't, I beat a hasty retreat. It was Katherine here who saw through my shaky performance."

I jam my hands on my hips. "Yes, I figured out it was you, me, the dumb Granger."

Mom looks surprised. "Dumb? With your good old-fashioned common sense? Hardly. You're our family problem solver and creative thinker. If I was on a desert island and was allowed one phone call to get me off, your number is the number I'd call." Mom looks me right in the eye and smiles her best real-life smile that brings out her dimples.

Mom's praise and warm smile dissolve my anger and puff me up. "I recognized your wave, Mom. No one waves like you. But what made me sure it was you was that box from Lombardo's that Suzanne brought to your room a couple of days ago. I thought it was your party dress, but tonight I remembered that Lombardo's is the costume shop where Annie and I rented our Halloween costumes last fall. That wasn't your dress in the box. It was your Abraham Lincoln costume, wasn't it?"

Though Mom doesn't answer, she laughs, which is proof enough. She hasn't laughed much since she's been president, and her laughter sounds good.

I haven't forgotten Mrs. B. "Where was Mrs. B.? I kept calling her, and she didn't come. Did she know what you were up to?"

Mom takes off her shawl. "Absolutely not. Do you want me to lose all credibility as a responsible adult? When your father and I came in from the reception, I told Mrs. Bruning that we'd keep an eye on you girls and she could go home. She missed out on all the fun."

Annie is still furious. "It wasn't fun, Mom."

That explains Mrs. B., but where was Robert? "What happened to Robert? He didn't come when I yelled, either."

Mom looks puzzled. "Who's Robert?"

"The agent on duty. He met me at the elevator after you left for the party and said he'd be outside the Lincoln Bedroom all night. So where was he?"

Dad knows all the Family Floor agents. "We don't have an agent named Robert that I know of. What's his last name?"

I couldn't come up with his last name if my life depended on it. Trust Annie to remember. "Todd. You told me his name was Robert Todd."

Dad thinks that one over. "Robert Todd?

That name sounds familiar. Do you know him, Margaret?"

Mom shakes her head. "No. Furthermore, I didn't request an agent. An agent outside the bedroom would have spoiled everything."

"Mmm . . . Robert Todd." Dad runs his hand over his bald spot, and then his face lights up. "No wonder the name sounds familiar. Robert Todd Lincoln was Abraham Lincoln's oldest son. . . ." His voice trails off. "Were you dreaming or what, KayKay?"

I'm so stunned that I don't answer.

Annie gets all excited. "That agent you saw was the moving man I told you about. He had a beard, and was tall and skinny and bald, wasn't he, KayKay? I told you I was right. He's the one, I know it."

I shake my head. "No way. Robert Todd has dark, slicked-down hair, a little mustache, and no beard. And he certainly wasn't tall and skinny. Wrong on every detail, Annie, but then you were hiding under the covers most of the time, so you never saw him."

This moving man has kept Annie hysterical

for weeks. Leave it to Dad to look into it. "I forgot to tell you, Annie, but I found out that man you keep talking about isn't a moving man at all. He's around, all right, but he's from the National Park Service and comes to the White House periodically to check the furnaces."

Annie looks almost disappointed, and because she doesn't like to look foolish she goes on the attack. "I bet anything you dreamed that agent up, just like Dad said, KayKay."

But I'm prepared. "Robert told me about Lincoln's two sons, who were always in trouble but never got punished. How could I dream that up?"

Mom and Dad exchange a look over my head. I know the look. It says that they'll go along with me for now, but they're sure my imagination has been playing tricks again.

I refuse to give in. "I did too see Robert. *And* talk to him."

Dad puts his arm around my shoulder. "Hey, you just had a big-time scare, KayKay. Why don't we drop it for tonight. For now, you and Annie can just chalk up the experience to that age-old saying that tonight your chickens came home to roost."

I don't get it. "What does that mean?"

"It means you and Annie became victims of a prank like the one you tried to pull on Matt. By the way, Matt dreamed up tonight's scenario before he left for Europe. He thought I should play Lincoln, but at five feet eight and a hundred and seventy pounds, I couldn't pass for Abraham Lincoln in a paper bag. Your Mother here surprised Matt and me by agreeing to do it."

Mom nods. "To tell the truth, I surprised myself. I guess I wanted to prove that I could be as good a sport as anyone."

Though my mind is still on Robert Todd, what Mom says catches me up short. "You mean things are going to be different from now on?"

All of a sudden, I can see Mom helping me with my mystery the way she used to help me with my schoolwork.

But Mom puts on the brakes. "Don't count on it. Even if I had time, I could never top my performance tonight . . . or want to. Anyway, it's been a night we'll all remember."

I'll go along with that. And from what I know about Abraham Lincoln, he might have had a good laugh himself. But make up some ghost story for Borden the way I'd planned? Or tell him what happened? No, family is as far as it will ever go.

Dad shifts to his favorite subject. "That midnight supper your mother and I had didn't do it for me, KayKay. How about whipping up some of your mushroom-and-onion omelettes? You could get started while we change."

Annie gets her order in. "Add extra onions, and don't forget the cheese."

Good, Annie and I are back on track. "Fine, as long as you set the table."

Mom starts to leave with Dad and then stops. "Incidentally, KayKay, if you ever call yourself 'dumb' again, I'll ground you for a month."

Just having Mom joke like that is a big step forward. An even bigger step is for Mom to call me KayKay again.

As I slice up the onions and mushrooms and drop them in the frying pan with butter, I get to thinking. Did I dream up Robert Todd? If that's the name of Abraham Lincoln's son, like Dad says, then maybe he was there to keep watch over his father's memory. But that's way too far-fetched, even by Annie's standards. Still, there's no way I could make up that name. I'll check the agent roster list tomorrow to see if Robert Todd is on it. Even if he is, I'm guessing I'll never see him again . . . or solve the mystery of who he is.

To be fair, the White House is more than two hundred years old, so why wouldn't it be filled with mysteries? No, *mysteries* isn't the right word. *Spirits* is more like it. Yes, that's what every president has left behind in the White House, not just furniture and china and portraits, but a spirit.

It's as if we Grangers are at the end of a long parade of spirits. Every president's family has left footprints in the White House, and I guess ours will, too. Though the White House will never be home to me the way our old house was, the last couple of weeks have showed me I can handle it.

But this is heavy thinking for the middle of the night. Right now, I have the cheese to grate and eggs to whisk so that the newest president, First Husband, and their two daughters can enjoy a middle-of-the-night picnic before the sun comes up and the White House rockets back to life.